Black Opal

Peri Jean Mace Ghost Thrillers #2

Copyright © 2016 Catie Rhodes.

Published by: Long Roads and Dark Ends Press

Cover artwork by Book Cover Corner

Content Editing by Word Webber Press

Copy Editing by The Independent Pen

Proofreading by Julie Glover

ISBN Ebook: 978-1-947462-04-5

ISBN Print: 978-1-947462-05-2

First Printing, 2013

Rhodes, Catie.

Black Opal/ Catie Rhodes. — 1st ed.

Visit the author website: www.catierhodes.com

SERIES LIST

Forever Road (Book #1)

Black Opal (Book #2)

Rocks & Gravel (Book #3)

Rest Stop (Book #4)

Forbidden Highway (Book #5)

Rear View: Prequel (Book #6)

Crossroads (Book #7)

Dead End (Book #8)

Dark Traveler (Book #9)

Wrong Turn (Book #10)

Last Exit (Book #11)

BLACK OPAL

PERI JEAN MACE GHOST THRILLERS #2

CATIE RHODES

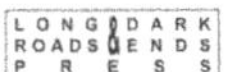

For my husband and family. Thank you for loving me just because.

1

——————

MY THROAT BURNED from too many cigarettes, but that didn't stop me from lighting my last one. The acrid smoke filling my vintage Chevy Nova fit my foul mood. Few kinds of trouble are more angst-ridden than boyfriend troubles.

"It's all your fault," I croaked at the troublemaking slip of paper fluttering in the fresh morning breeze. The offending piece of paper came from Wolfgang Puck's Five Sixty in Dallas and listed two of every item, including champagne. The tip and final total were written in Dean's blocky handwriting. I didn't know who he took there, but he sure as hell didn't take me.

Maybe I need to back up. This all started when Dean Turgeau's father, a man never spoken of before yesterday, broke his arm and had a heart attack scare. My boyfriend of six months took leave from his job as a sheriff's deputy in Gaslight City, Texas, and rushed to his hometown in South Louisiana. A few hours later, I got a hysterical phone call from him. Well, hysterical for Dean, anyway. For once, he sounded like he didn't know exactly how to control a situation.

"You gotta help me." He paused, breathing hard.

"What is it? Did you have an accident?" Fear kicked my imagination into high gear. Perhaps this was really Dean's ghost calling me. After all, my connection with the spirit world created more problems than it solved.

"No, no. It's my wallet. I forgot it, and I just spent my emergency cash on gas. I have no ID, no credit cards, nothing." His voice wavered on the last word.

I nodded and then remembered he couldn't see me. This wasn't about the wallet at all. It was about Dean, the most in-control man I'd ever met, losing control. No doubt he feared losing his father. Caring for my terminally ill grandmother, the only family I had left, made me hyper-aware of such things.

"Hey, it's all right. I'll overnight it to you. Use that key you gave me," I said. Dean had given me an extravagantly wrapped key to his house. Now would be the perfect time to break it in. Whatever response I expected was a far cry from the one I got: complete, total, and utter silence. After a long enough pause for me to regret offering, Dean finally stuttered out a few words.

"Y-yeah. I guess that's fine." He trailed off but came back sounding more confident. "Sure. Do that." He rattled off an address in Louisiana. Busy writing it down, I never stopped to think about his weird reaction until I found the receipt.

My search for a box and tape took me to the detached

garage. The first thing I saw in there sent my suspicions into a tailspin. Dean's vintage Smokey and the Bandit era Trans-Am sat in the middle of the stifling little room. The sight threw me for a loop, the kind where I felt my stomach fall thirteen floors. The Trans-Am was—to the best of my knowledge—Dean's only car. So what did he drive to Louisiana? Looking for some answers, or maybe just being nosy, I slid into the Trans-Am and opened the glove box. The receipt fluttered out, setting the stage for a mega meltdown.

Seething, I wrapped the wallet like a gift, complete with white paper and a curlicue green ribbon. I resisted the urge to put the receipt in the box like a cherry on top of Dean's wallet. Then I packed a bag, got in my car, and drove most of the night.

Now I was close to the end of my three-hundred-mile journey with no clear idea what I wanted to say to Dean. My pissed off level hovered in the red. Between that and eating no food since I found the receipt, my stomach sizzled and burned. I felt miserable and would be until Dean Turgeau gave me an explanation.

The lush South Louisiana landscape unfurled like a flower, growing more exotic and mysterious as I drove deeper into the state. But I had a hard time enjoying it. The trees draped with Spanish moss brought to mind romance novel covers, which just added to the whole pissed off thing. Views stretching out into tree-studded bayous looked like postcards advertising an enchanting weekend getaway. My mind supplied endless ideas about who Dean really came down here to see.

After all, he left his prized 1980s Trans-Am in his garage back in Gaslight City. Maybe his other girlfriend didn't like vintage cars. Maybe she drove them here. *What a fool you are not to have seen this coming, Peri Jean Mace.* Feeling foolish nestled at the root of my anger. I did everything I could not to let people make a fool of me. *Look at me now.*

I thought I'd learned to read Dean over the past six months. So much for my intuition. Now I saw the error in my thinking. When a man, one I thought I might love, gave me a key to his house in a gold box with a purple ribbon tied around it, that really meant I needed to watch out. *How could you be so dumb?* I crumpled the receipt and shoved it in my pocket. I'd know next time.

I exited I-10 south of Baton Rouge, still practicing how I'd confront Dean, and did a double take at the change in scenery. Clear-cut farmland, the ground turned to expose the fertile black soil, stretched into the distance and a white haze of humidity floated like a premonition on the horizon. Roadside signs advertising historic plantations loomed over dilapidated shacks. Boarded up gas stations, their wood grayed and bowed, lingered forgotten in overgrown fields. Glimpses of the grand Mississippi twinkled in the distance, peeking through the dense trees.

So this is where Dean grew up, in this mysterious world of shadows and contrast. This is where he learned how to love, hate, and buy expensive, clandestine dinners for persons unknown. Mind reeling, I pulled into a gas station to buy more cigarettes, ask directions, and fuel up.

BACK IN MY CAR, I drove along at a snail's pace, looking for a white brick mailbox.

"You can't miss it, ma'am. Biggest mailbox I ever seen." The gas station attendant's drawl rolled over the vowels in a way mine didn't and made me feel farther from home than all the miles of highway put together.

The road followed the bend of the river, undulating and winding lazily along. My impatience to get this show on the road made me want to drive faster, but I didn't dare. Rounding a sharp curve, I came up behind a young woman, maybe a teenager, walking in the grass on the roadside. *What the hell?* I pulled into the middle of the road to give her plenty of room.

This chick looked like she'd gotten on the wrong side of something or other. Black streaks and cuts ran up and down her legs, and the bottoms of her bare feet matched the road. I spotted a gash on one of them. She held her head at a funny angle, as though it hurt. It didn't take a degree in rocket science to know something was wrong.

I slowed even more, traveling at nearly a crawl. The desire to stop and offer my help was almost too strong to resist. Common sense kept me from acting on it. *I am a woman traveling alone in a strange state, in a strange town.* Leaving the address with my terminally ill grandmother didn't count when she was three hundred miles away. I drew alongside the girl and leaned over the seat to look at her. She walked staring straight ahead. *Can't she see and hear my car creeping along beside her?*

A horn tooted and jerked my attention back to the road. The driver of an approaching truck glared at me from behind the windshield, evidently wanting his share of the road. Irritation flashed. *Doesn't he see this girl is in a bad way?* I glanced back at the girl, ready to shake my fist at the truck driver, but she had disappeared. Instead, I saw the white mailbox.

The gas station attendant didn't lie. It would have been impossible to miss. The mailbox, built of white-painted brick, resembled a turret on a castle. The pea gravel driveway was right next to it. It was either turn now or miss it altogether, and this road didn't have too many places to turn around. I didn't have time to think about where the teenage girl went so fast.

I whipped into the driveway, the tiny rocks rolling and popping under my tires. The driveway traveled at an incline, so I couldn't see the house right away. When I got to the top of a little hill, a big, white elephant of a house unfolded in front of me. I jammed on the breaks and gaped at it.

"You have got to be kidding me," I said to the empty car.

Four columns ran across the front, framing a second-story balcony. The monstrosity sat on a brick foundation taller than a man, topped by a porch running the entire length of the house's front. Elaborate wrought-iron railings embraced two sets of curved steps, one on each end of the porch. The windows lining the house's front stood at least ten feet tall and sported stained glass panes of blue and purple at their tops. One word came to mind:

never-ending. Everywhere I looked there was more house.

"Holy shit." I counted four chimneys rising from different parts of the house, each adorned with elaborate masonry designs around the top. Every piece of the house was just so. I saw not an inch of flaking paint or even one board that looked rotted. *Who has money for something like this?* A blacktopped parking lot surrounded by a wrought-iron fence sat a distance from the house. I pulled in and parked, shocked by the cars. The least expensive was a new Cadillac SUV. I fumbled another cigarette into my mouth, hoping it would cool off my perception of all this. It couldn't be all that bad. But it sure looked like it was.

The house and grounds looked like a TV remake of *Cat on a Hot Tin Roof.* These folks would take one look at me and tell me to get lost. For a moment, I forgot the receipt and the sickening mixture of humiliation and anger I felt over it. It might not be the worst my day had to offer. These folks might get security to escort me from the premises.

Where the hell is Dean in all this? The only logical conclusion was Dean's family worked here. He said his father got hurt clearing debris washed up by a flood. Sure enough, branches, leaves, and other nature-produced garbage littered the lush, perfectly manicured grounds. Cleaning this up would be no small chore.

I let the huge house intimidate me a moment longer before I grabbed Dean's gift-wrapped wallet and forced myself out of my beat-up old Nova. I had no idea how to approach a place like this and inquire after people I thought might work here. Was it appropriate for me to knock on the back door? Surely not in the twenty-first century. I loitered next to my car, frozen with uncertainty.

"I knowed you'd be coming." The voice came from next to my arm, male but high and reedy. I jerked in surprise and twisted around. The man was around Dean's age—pushing forty—and balding with wispy hair stuck to his head. I recognized the bulbous, broken-veined nose of a drinker. Patchy stubble covered his face. "You here to make things right, ain't you?"

I recoiled from him, uncertain how to respond. Nobody expected me. And, even if they did, make what things right? *That girl on the highway.* The image of her popped into my head like a monster coming out of hiding. A chill worked its way through the thick humidity and settled over me. *Oh, hell no. Not this shit again.*

The man crowded toward me, coming so close I smelled his booze sweat and something else, something animal. He leaned into my face and stared into my eyes. I tried to back away but my butt bumped my car. Trapped by this weirdo, fear zinged through my veins as the adrenaline kicked in. I swung my head side to side. I wanted to end this crazy encounter. But I saw no way out.

THE MAN EXHALED in my face, and the foul odor shot up my nose. Rotted teeth and some kind of alcohol. Fuck being polite. I shoved him away from me. He went willingly enough but only a few feet.

"You see 'em, don't you? The dead, I mean." He swayed like someone who just got off a train or a boat.

My mouth went dry. The madness in this man's eyes could well be from seeing the other side. My life's fear was going mad, maybe losing myself to drugs or drink, and becoming like this trembling, incoherent creature in front of me.

"Trey?" The voice came from shadows created by a small copse of trees next to the parking area. I squinted into the gloom, heart pounding, praying this weird little man hadn't brought the wrath of some crazy ghost down on me.

Trey backed away from me, glancing furtively in the direction of the voice. Its owner's footsteps crunched in the litter of branches, leaves, and uprooted vegetation, the shadows playing over his face until he was upon us. I had to crane my neck to look up at him and almost gasped at his beauty.

There are good-looking men, and there are beautiful men. This guy was one of the latter. Tall, lean, and tawny skinned, his square jaw framed high cheekbones. Dirty blond hair set off bright aqua eyes. He walked at a languid pace, as though daring anything or anybody to ask him to hurry. When he reached Trey, he gripped the shorter man's arm and yanked him away from me.

"Why are you bothering visitors?" His accent played like music, educated but full of drawn out syllables and soft consonants. Like the gas station attendant's, only more toe curling. "You get on back to the barn where you belong now."

Trey lowered his head and scurried away. Gorgeous and I stared at each other. My heart belonged to Dean, but I'd have to be blind—hell, dead—not to appreciate this guy.

"I'm sorry about that," he said. It was all I could do not to curtsy.

"I hate to admit it, but he scared me." Just those few words had a coquettish lilt to them. Ugh. I liked 'em pretty, but this was ridiculous. Even for me.

"Don't mind him. He's not right in the head," Gorgeous said. "You here to see someone?"

"Dean Turgeau?" I heard the question mark after Dean's name and winced. I sounded like a flirty southern belle out for a hot afternoon with a gentlemanly stranger.

"Just go right on up to the house, ma'am. They'll help you find him." Gorgeous half-waved and disappeared back into shadowy trees.

I bet his family owned this place, and he supervised the workers. He had that air about him, the gentleman son of old money. Had he stayed to chat, I suspect I'd have made a fool of myself. One more gander at the imposing house, and I shook off my thoughts and marched up to the front door. I couldn't tell where my huff over the receipt ended and my dread of encountering the mansion's inhabitants began.

I punched the doorbell and heard a loud gong in the house. Quickly—so quickly I assumed the woman who answered must have been standing on the other side—the door swung open. The middle-aged woman wore an old-fashioned black and white maid's uniform. I gaped, never having seen one outside television. She stood in the doorway, a mildly inquiring expression on her face.

"Help you?" She didn't bother to smile. *Goody. This was going just as I thought.* I wondered how to address her. She looked young to be Dean's mother, but I couldn't think fast enough to figure out who else she might be.

"Mrs. Turgeau?"

The woman tried to hold in her laugher. That just made it escape in snickers and snorts. Heat burned my cheeks, and I didn't need a mirror to know my head looked like an extra large cherry with black hair. The woman took in my embarrassment and clapped her hands over her mouth. I considered making a run for it.

GLANCING over my shoulder at the blacktopped parking lot and my car, I calculated the number of seconds it would take to reach it and how many steps I'd have to take before I could no longer see the woman's amusement. That held highest priority. It reminded me too much of my school years.

A voice came from within the house, "Nadine, who's at the door? If it's Father Reilly, send him back."

Nadine took her hand off her mouth to speak. "No, ma'am. I think it's for you."

"Fine," the voice said, "I'll be out in a moment. Show them into the foyer and close the door before the house fills with bugs."

Throughout this exchange, my mortification intensified. I knew whatever was about to happen would end with me looking like the biggest idiot in the world.

Nadine looked me up and down. For the first time since I chose my traveling clothes, I became aware of the faded t-shirt with the crusty rock band emblem still clinging to it and the cut-off blue jean shorts I wore. She muttered under her breath, but loud enough for me to hear, "Unbelievable. Come on in."

The tap-tap of high heels rang on the pinkish marble floor. From the sound of it, more than one person was on the way to greet me.

A woman who could have been on the cover of a magazine entered first. She wore her shining dark hair long and in a style that must have taken hours and required complex tools to create. Her makeup was one of those complicated jobs designed to make her look younger, with very light colors surrounding her eyes. She took one look at me, wrinkled her nose, and quickly covered it with a 'possum grin.

An older woman sauntered into the foyer behind her, and I suddenly understood what amused Nadine the maid so much. It only took one glance to know this was Dean's mother or a very close relative. *What next, universe?* The oval face, the straight bridge of her nose, the full lips, and dimpled chin resembled Dean so strongly, it was eerie. This woman walked at a pace saying she didn't have to hurry for anybody. Diamonds and rubies twinkled at both ears and at her throat. She glanced at Nadine, who still giggled with her hand over her mouth, and cocked her head to one side. Even her demeanor was Dean at his haughtiest.

Oh lordy, Peri Jean. Just what have you gotten yourself into this time?

"This must be Dean's girlfriend we've all been waiting on. She thought I was you. " Nadine chuckled again but, when she saw Mrs. Turgeau did not share her amusement, cut it off.

Dean's girlfriend? Were they expecting me? The lady of the manor continued to stare at Nadine, her face still and impassive, until Nadine scurried out of the room. Then she walked toward me, a smile curving her lips and crinkling her eyes. Also like Dean, she seemed to switch emotions on a dime. She held out her hand. My heart thudded so hard, I worried it might jump out of my mouth if I spoke. I kept my lips firmly sealed just in case.

"You must be Peri Jean. Your grandmother called Dean and told him to expect you. I'm Julienne Turgeau, Dean's mother." We shook. I could do no more than gulp and nod.

A college-aged woman wearing a sweat-ringed tank top and running shorts sped into the room, her eyes comically wide. Her workout shoes squeaked as she came to a sudden stop on the marble floor. She studied me from my canvas lace-up shoes to my short pixie cut. Her lips, a feminine version of Dean's, curved into a smile, and she stuck out her hand.

"I'm Maddy—Madeleine, that is—Dean's baby sister."

"Peri Jean. Dean's girlfriend." I couldn't help but return her smile as I gripped her sweaty hand in a brief handshake.

The other woman, who I guessed was another of Dean's sisters by her age, stepped forward and held out her hand. "I am Lisette David-Turgeau-Carter. I was Dean's wife for about fifteen years."

Every cigarette I smoked on the trip picked that moment to make me gag and cough. The receipt from Five Sixty in Dallas flashed in my memory, and things clicked into place. Taking a bath in buffalo doo doo would have had more appeal than living through the next few minutes.

2

———

DEAN'S MOTHER ushered us into a room she called the parlor. The air smelled like polished wood and antiques and money. The little details, like the faux columns set into the walls adorned with elaborate carvings, highlighted the differences between this world and mine back in Gaslight City, Texas.

I couldn't help but stare at the fancy trim running around the edges of the high ceiling. It reminded me of tiers on a high-dollar wedding cake. Nadine, who gave me a sideways glance, set a silver tea set on a Queen Anne style tea table. *Screw style. I bet that table is the real deal and worth thousands of dollars.*

The more I took in all the details, the more hurt and scared I felt. *Did Dean just forget to tell me about all this? My ass, he did.* As usual, my hurt and fear defaulted to satisfying, blistering anger. I'd only thought myself angry about the receipt. Dean's omission of this place and the people in it infuriated me.

Movement outside the open door caught my eye, and I stared at the area, halfway expecting yet another relative to join us. The stained glass window from which the hallway got most of its light cast the area in a surreal, funhouse glow. About the time I decided I'd seen nothing, something flashed through the area again. I opened my second sight in time to glimpse the girl I'd seen on the road. The one who had been in a scuffle.

This close, she gave off a feeling I knew well. The hair on my arms raised, and I suppressed a shiver. It hadn't taken long at all for the dead to find me. *Great. Just great. If my luck held, these people would find out I see ghosts and ostracize me just like people have all my life.* Realizing my worries had taken on a fever pitch, I forced them to a stop, focused on the living occupants of the room, and took deep breaths.

Dean's ex-wife and his sister settled down on a Victorian courting couch. *Bet it's original to the house.*

Looking at Lisette, I believed more than ever she'd shared an elegant meal with him in the revolving restaurant atop Reunion Tower in Dallas. There was no way I could compete with her creamy, unmarred skin, her shining, expensively styled hair, or her sophisticated outfit. My cuteness was a honky-tonk guitar to her symphony of beauty. She held my eyes with an expression I couldn't quite decipher.

"You sit right here next to me, Peri Jean." Mrs. Turgeau patted the spot next to her on an expensively upholstered love seat. I ran my hand over the fabric, feeling the bumps of the raised floral pattern. *Please don't let me spill anything.*

Mrs. Turgeau and the ex-wife each took a treat and nibbled daintily. The sister waved the treats away with a smile. I resisted the urge to grab huge handfuls and shove them into my mouth just to be obnoxious. I needed to do something to feel in control of the situation, so I started running my mouth.

"Your home is amazing." I twisted in my seat to peer at a Tiffany lamp on the end table. I stopped when I realized they all watched me, eyebrows raised, with varying degrees of curiosity. "Is this the Venetian pattern?"

Dean's ex-wife leaned forward. "Very good. I can never keep all the patterns straight."

She surprised me. If she was seeing Dean, wouldn't she act catty and jealous?

"That one dates back to the 1920s," Julienne said. "My grandmother, Fayette, purchased it. Do you know Tiffany lamps?"

"Only a little. Sometimes I fill in at an antique store. I hear the names of stuff, but I've never owned any of it myself."

Dean's ex nodded in understanding even though she looked like she had a houseful of Tiffany lamps.

"This home has been in my family since 1825," Julienne Turgeau said with a smile she probably intended to put me at ease. It only made my guts grind tighter. "I don't know if I'd own half the items in it had they not been hand-me-downs."

"Did you see them in concert?" Dean's sister spoke for the first time since she introduced herself, gesturing at my t-shirt.

"A long time ago." We exchanged smiles. "They were good."

"Dean and I went to see them once." Lisette's voice sounded soft, cultured. It reminded me of the man I met in the parking lot. I started to ask about him, but once Dean's ex got talking, it seemed like she couldn't shut up. "We were living in Florida. Dean was in law school, and I was trying to get pregnant."

Law school? Pregnant? Holy feral cats. For the first time, I felt the weight of Dean's and my ten-year age difference. He'd lived a whole life while I grew up. Suppressing a gulp, I took a deep breath and hoped my shock didn't show on my face.

Madeleine took one look at me and winced. "I wanted you to join me and Dean in Dallas for dinner on my birthday, but he said you had something else going on." She gave me a small smile, making me think she'd changed subject on purpose.

"Where'd y'all go?" I tried to keep my voice even, but my whirling thoughts made it difficult.

"Five Sixty. It's at the top of Reunion Tower. They have Asian food." She grinned. "Dean bought me champagne."

Oh no. My nervousness morphed into relief, then embarrassment, and back into nervousness. I clutched my stomach, trying to keep the stampede inside. I couldn't even formulate an answer. I'd driven three hundred miles, found out things about Dean I wished I didn't know, and it was all over me jumping to conclusions. *At least I've got a legitimate reason to be here. Sort of.*

"IT'S VERY nice of you to hand-deliver my son's wallet." Julienne Turgeau crossed her legs and straightened her light blue pantsuit. The suit and coordinating shoes matched the eye color she shared with her son. She gave me another kind smile and the barest of winks. *Did she somehow know I came here to give Dean the what-for? How mortifying.*

I acknowledged her thanks with a nod. "Dean was upset about it."

Julienne nodded and took a sip of her tea. "My younger son takes life very, very seriously."

We shared a smile. My mood lightened a bit...until Dean's ex piped up. "Dean got that way after our divorce. He used to be really fun."

I ignored Lisette and spoke directly to Julienne. "Where is Dean?"

Lisette narrowed her eyes at me, her nostrils flaring. Now that I knew Dean's dinner at Five Sixty was a birthday present to his sister, I wondered what the hell his ex-wife was doing here.

"He and his older brother are outside trying to join their father in the hospital." Julienne set her tea cup on the tray and took out her cell phone. "I'll let him know you're here." Her fingers flew over the display, and I heard the familiar swoosh sound as she sent her text message.

"Thanks." I bit into something totally unfamiliar. "I'm sorry to hear of your husband's accident."

"I told Big Rick a hundred times he's too old to be out

there working alongside the younger men. But he thinks not doing it would mean he's getting old—which he is—so he never listens." She pursed her lips. "He scared all of us. Then the old goat tried to leave the hospital, and that started another panic. The doctors expect him to make a full recovery."

"I hope I'm not keeping you from visiting him at the hospital." Actually, I hoped I was. Then maybe I could get out of this uncomfortable situation.

"Oh, dear, no." Julienne laughed. "Rick's used to being the boss, and he can't stand not being in charge at the hospital. I'd prefer not to see all the awful fits he pulls."

"Daddy made one of the nurses cry yesterday," said Madeleine.

A few months ago, I'd have been horrified and classified Dean's father as someone I'd prefer not to meet. But the last several months of dealing with Memaw's failing health had opened my eyes to a whole new world. Some people didn't have the patience to be patients. A little stab of guilt for leaving Memaw alone worked its way into me, even though her doctor promised to check in on her.

"Remember when Big Rick got food poisoning from that roadside stand?" Lisette's dark eyes met and held Julienne's.

"Do I ever," the older woman laughed. "I thought he would go into shock and die before he let us take him to the hospital."

"Lisette grew up with my older children," Julienne told me. "Her mother had...health problems, and we sort of took her in."

Lisette glanced at me, silently asking if I understood she'd been around way longer than I had. I dropped my gaze to my feet. It wasn't in my nature to back down, but this place had me off my game. Nothing was as I'd imagined. I wished I could take back the decision to come storming into Dean's life. Had a black hole to nowhere opened in the floor, I would've swan dived into its depths. Feeling eyes on me, I glanced up. Lisette beamed at me.

"Health problems?" Lisette snorted, still smiling like she'd just won something big. I guess she had. "She was a mean-mouthed lush."

Dean's mother flushed, and his sister looked at her watch. The sound of a door opening interrupted our uncomfortable silence. Dean's voice echoed through the house. "Mom?"

"We're in the parlor, son. Take off your shoes and leave them outside the door." Dean's mother flashed another smile at me. I made myself smile back even though regret hung over me like a dark cloud. *You should have stayed home, girl. Oh well. Another stupid decision in a life full of 'em.*

DEAN PADDED INTO THE ROOM, sweaty, dirty, and shoeless. He grinned when he saw me and said, "Isn't it usually you who looks like you crawled through a mile of mud?"

I felt an unwanted little bolt of joy at seeing Dean. Then I reminded myself to be annoyed. Dean's family, while nice enough, were wealthy beyond what I could comprehend. His choice not to tell me about them didn't look or feel good. *I shouldn't have come here.*

Madeleine tugged Dean's arm and crossed her eyes at him. He arranged his face into an expression of mock outrage and stuck his nose into the air. Formalities complete, he crossed the room, heading straight for me.

"Don't touch the furniture." Julienne held up one finger, a gesture that had more command than any amount of shouting she could have done.

I stood, butterflies turning somersaults in my stomach. Somehow I expected him to act different now. I knew his secret. But he held his arms open to me, and, forgetting my irritation with him, I hugged him tight. He pulled back from me, his eyes twinkling, obviously thrilled to see me. *If he didn't mind me showing up, why didn't he tell me about these people?*

"I'm so glad you're here." He inhaled deeply and squeezed me again. "I thought my nosy mother and sister would drive me crazy asking questions about you."

Feeling eyes on me, I glanced up to find Lisette glaring at me, hectic spots of red flaming on her high cheekbones. *Now that's more like it.* Was her frequent presence what kept Dean quiet about his family? He said their marriage went down in flames. The details I knew made it surprising she still showed her face here.

I glanced at Dean, hoping for a hint of the situation between them, but he was engaged in and exchange of nonverbal insults with his sister. Now that I thought about it, he hadn't even acknowledged Lisette. Her eyes followed every move he made, though. She caught me looking at her and immediately switched back to her cool as a cucumber routine. *Interesting. Chick's a hell of an actress.* I ignored her to watch Dean's and Madeleine's antics. This side of him was almost charming.

"Don't do that to her," I said. "It might warp her for life." Everybody, except Lisette, laughed. I retrieved the box holding Dean's wallet and gave it to him. Using a pocket knife, he cut open the box as though it was a special gift. Lisette made Godzilla eyes at us. I made a point to keep my back turned to her, letting her know she didn't scare me.

"You don't know how much I appreciate this." Dean glanced at one of the brocade-covered love seats and received a look from his mother so scathing it burned even me. He shuffled foot to foot.

"Let's just go outside. Your mother has enough to worry about without you filthying the house." I wanted to get him alone so I could find out why he never told me he was richer than the richest people I knew, why he didn't invite me to his sister's birthday dinner, and what vehicle he drove here to richie-ville. Not knowing those things made me wonder if Dean considered me more of a friend with benefits than a girlfriend. Had I misread our relationship? I didn't like the feeling of horror creeping over me at this thought.

Dean led me through an open room bigger than the house I shared with Memaw. The crystal chandelier hanging many feet overhead looked as big as my bed. Dean pulled my arm and motioned me into a dark passage.

"What is this?"

"Servant's passage. They're all over this house."

"This place is massive." I still couldn't wrap my head around Dean growing up here.

"This old monstrosity has seventy-five rooms." He pulled me through the passage, which ended at a closed door. Dean pushed it open, and we exited onto the turreted wing I noticed when I arrived. "There are sections of the attic I've never even ventured into."

Part of me wanted to let all the things that didn't add up fall by the wayside, have a nice visit with Dean, and drive back to Texas. But, now, I'd planted seeds of doubt in my own mind. I had to know why he'd worked so hard to keep me away from this side of his life. Embarrassment? If so, we could end things right here. *Maybe he just ain't that into you, Peri Jean.* I cringed.

Dean sat on the stone steps and slid his feet into lace-up hiking boots. Feeling my stare, he twisted to look at me. He frowned at whatever he saw on my face. "Let's get away from the house before you let loose on me."

3
—————

DEAN LED me away from the house and the workers on the lawn. A few of them popped their heads up to watch us walking. Neither of us spoke. Tense with anger and trepidation, I wrung my hands. The cloud-filled sky darkened to the color of bruises and thunder boomed in the distance. Dean gazed at the horizon and heaved a sigh.

"Come on," he said. "Let's get this over with. You're pissed because Lisette's here, right?"

"Is that what you think?" I rolled my eyes, knowing it would ignite Dean's fury. "This is about secrets. Your secrets."

"Secrets?" His eyes widened and darted back at the house. "What secrets?"

He knew exactly what secrets I meant. His babe in the woods routine would not work on me.

"I saw your Trans-Am in the garage when I picked up your wallet. How'd you get here?" *Did he expect me to believe he friggin' walked?*

"I drove." Dean furrowed his brow.

Boy that told me a lot. "Exactly *what* did you drive?"

Dean glanced at my forty-year-old Nova in the fenced-in parking area and gestured at the BMW sitting next to it. "That's my other car. The dependable one."

"You never told me you had two cars. Why?"

"I didn't realize it was a big deal." Dean shoved his hands in his pockets and picked up the pace. *Liar. He knew it would be a big deal to me. Otherwise, he'd have mentioned it.*

I tagged after him, the silence growing more tense with each step. Thunder rumbled, and I smelled rain coming. Dean and I passed tennis courts, an Olympic-sized swimming pool complete with a guesthouse, and stopped at a huge structure I assumed was a horse barn. The opulence annoyed me all the more. Why had Dean put a curtain up between his two lives? The first drops of rain slapped the already saturated ground, and he pulled me into the huge structure.

"The damn car doesn't matter, and you know it. What's crawled up your ass?" He put his hands on his hips and narrowed his eyes at me.

"We've been dating for six months, and you never told me about this?" I swept my arms wide. "Hell, you never even mentioned your family. Your sister said she asked you to include me in her birthday dinner. You didn't do it. Why?" My shame came rushing back, and I wanted to curl up, to lick my wounds, to run away. "Are you ashamed of me?"

"Oh, come on. The timing hasn't been right." He crossed his arms over his chest, completely ignoring the question I asked. "Your grandmother's cancer has you stressed. You're so tired you can barely take care of your business. Can you honestly tell me you'd have welcomed meeting my family in the middle of all that?"

"Maddy said she wanted to meet me, but you never even mentioned it to me. You could have let me make my own choice."

"I was spending the night, getting a hotel room." He spoke through clenched teeth and balled his hands into fists so veins stood out in his arms. "Since you refuse to spend a whole night in the same bed with me, I didn't want to put you on the spot."

I jerked, wanting to crawl under the worn boards at my feet. I couldn't have looked like a bigger jackass if I'd planned it. Over the past six months, Dean had hinted, joked, and finally given me the key to his house to make clear he wanted me to spend the night. And I couldn't. Just couldn't.

When things got quiet, I itched to go home, sleep in my own bed. In some dark, hidden part of my mind, I thought not spending the night with Dean might keep him from hurting me. Because, in the end, they all left—my father, my mother, my ex-husband, my friends. It wasn't that I kept my feelings secret. There was no way to make him understand.

A board creaked overhead. Dean and I both peered into the open loft to see a man looking down at us. I gasped. It was the same drunk who confronted me in the parking lot. He climbed out of the loft and walked toward us.

I BACKED AWAY. Dean frowned at my reaction and stepped in front of me, separating me from the stranger. The man—what did Beautiful call him? Trey?—took slow steps toward us, his hands held out in front of him.

"Miss, I am so sorry I upset you earlier. Sometimes my drinking gets the best of me."

I moved closer to Dean until my hip bumped him. He reached one arm behind him and held it across me, as though one arm could protect me if this guy attacked us. Something about the man felt off, and he scared me. Had I been alone, I'd have thought both he and the gorgeous man I met earlier were ghosts, that the fuckers had now gained the ability to speak with me.

"What's going on here?" Dean kept himself between the man and me.

"I scared your girl in the parking area." A mottled red flush spread down Trey's neck and disappeared into his shirt. Pity washed over me. I didn't want to get this sick little man in trouble.

"I overreacted...Trey? Is that it?" I peeked around Dean.

Twisting his baseball cap in his hands, Trey ventured a glance at my face and nodded.

"Forgive me, Trey. I was in an unfamiliar place, and you surprised me."

Trey nodded and turned his attention to Dean. "Hate to say it, but y'all getting sort of loud. Horses don't like it. With the storm outside, they're a little jumpy."

"No problem." Dean motioned me to follow him from the barn.

Even the dark sky didn't hide the anger etched into Dean's face. Cold rain pattered down on us, chilling me and adding to my foul mood. Before I could voice a smart-assed remark and make things worse, he said, "I wanted to tell you about my family, introduce you to them, but I didn't know if you wanted to take that step."

He meant because I wouldn't spend the night with him. I guessed he wondered where he stood with me. Same thing I wondered about him. I gulped but said nothing. If Dean was guilty of putting a curtain between me and this other life of his, I was guilty of keeping myself separate from him.

"Peri Jean, I can't do this indefinitely." Dean glanced at the fenced parking lot where his fancy BMW sat next to my old clunker and wiped the rain off his face. "There are things I love about you, but this isn't one of them."

My face heated, and my words came out swinging. "Can't keep doing what?"

"Walking on eggshells for you. I know you've got trust issues, and I get it. But I can't ride through one of your upheavals every time something scares you."

My toes curled as embarrassment stung me. *Do I freak out that often? But who is he to talk about trust issues? I do a good deal of tiptoeing around for him, too.*

"Like you're well-adjusted. Before yesterday, I thought you were either estranged from your parents or they were no longer living. And you're riding my ass about trust?"

"Okay. Neither of us is easy. Point taken." Dean held

out both hands. He shook his head and let out a sigh. "All this is why I cringed when Memaw called and said you were on the way. I knew you'd see all this, see Lisette here, and feel insecure."

"Insecure? Is that how you see me?" My blood boiled at his condescension, even though I knew he was right. "Fuck this. I'm sorry I bothered." I started walking.

"That's it, babe, keep walking," he called after me. "Every time something catches you off guard, you pitch a fit and walk away. Look how much good it does you."

The storm of nerves tingling in my stomach and face intensified, and I whipped around. "That is not true. Because if it were, I'd have walked away from you and your moods a dozen times."

"Like it's pleasant to deal with thirty years of baggage that comes out as paranoia and wanting to hurt people before they hurt you." Dean's eyes narrowed into mean slits. He was done trying to cajole me. Well, I was done, too.

"And you never do shit like that." I remembered the first few conversations we had after he learned I communicated with the dead. He treated me like a leper.

"Let's just do this some other time." He closed his eyes. "Please?"

"Fine. I'll see you back in Texas." I started the walk back to my car, the miserable rain slapping against me and my heart aching.

Dean, obviously as angry as I was, applauded me as I walked. I flipped him the one-fingered salute over my shoulder.

"Shit," he said. "Peri Jean, wait. Just wait."

I kept walking.

DEAN HURRIED AFTER ME, grunting as the uneven ground took its toll on an old shooting injury he'd gotten in the line of duty. Had I not been angry, I'd have slowed down for him. But his words hit me where it hurt. I walked to my car as fast as my short legs would go, unlocked it, and got in. Dean took the last few steps running and stood in the open door.

"Don't leave like this." His eyes, the windows of his soul, pleaded. I was too angry at him for calling me on my insecurity to show him any mercy. I started the car.

"If you don't move, I'm going to put this car in reverse and drag you down the driveway."

I saw the hurt and anger ignite in Dean's eyes. An answering ache throbbed in my chest. I didn't want to leave things right here, but my pride was too big. I let off the brake, and the car eased backward. Dean jumped out of the way.

I turned the car around and headed back the way I came. A glance in my rearview mirror showed me Dean looking lost and bewildered. A tall, elegant figure stood in the open front door. The cloud of dark hair told me it was Lisette. *That bitch can just have him.*

The car picked up speed as I coasted down the drive-way. I tapped the brake and got no response. I hit the brake pedal harder. The car didn't even slow. Panic squeezed my chest and clawed its way up my throat. My mind kicked into warp speed, scrambling over the options.

I couldn't make the hairpin turn onto the road. I'd hit the levee separating the river from the road. The impact might kill me. I stomped the brake pedal again. It wouldn't do me any good. I knew that. But I had to try it. I glanced down at my feet to make sure nothing obstructed the brake pedal. It was clear.

When I straightened, a figure stood in my path. My endorphin soaked mind ratcheted up the level of horror coursing through me. Then I recognized the girl from the road, the same one I saw in the house. *The ghost.* My car barreled straight at her. I had only seconds to act. Dead or not, I couldn't just hit her. Without further consideration, I drove my car into a drainage ditch.

My car, the only thing I had left of my father, hit the mud with a heartbreaking splat and stalled. I flew forward and smacked my head on the driver side window. The pain stunned me, but my worries centered more on the car than on my own health. I loved this car. It made me feel like I had some connection to my dead father, even though I didn't.

Splashing sounds jerked me out of my pity party. I turned to see Dean scrambling down the banks of the ditch, using roots to control his descent. He wiped the mud off my window and tapped on it. I rolled it down as though we were in a parking lot somewhere.

"Are you okay? Is anything hurt? Can you breathe?" When I said nothing, he grabbed my shoulder and gave me a hard shake. "Peri Jean? Can you talk?"

"I can talk. I was just waiting for you to finish."

Dean exhaled hard through his nostrils. He muttered under his breath but kept it loud enough for me to hear. "I don't understand why you have to be such a smartass."

I don't either. It just makes things worse. Instead of saying that I turned away from him.

"You all right down there?" The creepy guy from the barn and another guy I recognized as one of the men working on the lawn peered into the ditch.

"I don't think she's hurt," Dean said.

"No, I'm not hurt," I said and climbed out of the car. The standing water covered my cheap canvas shoes, and I started shivering. I looked around for the ghost. She made me crash because she wanted me here. I didn't have to be a genius to know that. Sooner than later, she'd let me know what she wanted. I wasn't looking forward to it. Dean accepted me seeing ghosts, knew it was real, but it bugged him. This would only complicate things between us more.

Another figure leaned over the edge of the ditch and looked at me. Lisette. Her dark eyes danced. The bitch was enjoying this.

4
———

DEAN CALLED A TOW TRUCK. The driver, who looked like a cross between a string bean and a ferret, only with grease, said, "Got three more cars before you, baby. Might get to it tomorrow. Mebbe the day after that, though."

"Are there any hotels near here or are they all in Baton Rouge?" I hoped not. Baton Rouge was forty minutes back the way I came. With Dean and I arguing, he might not give me a ride. And how would I get back here to get my car?

"You're not staying at a hotel." Julienne crossed her arms over her chest. "I'll be insulted if you don't stay in my home."

What could I say? No way I'd admit Dean and I were engaged in battle, not with smug-faced Lisette standing right there. Dean's mother assigned Madeleine to settle me in as a guest. That's how I found myself following the younger woman all over the huge house while she gathered towels from a well-stocked linen closet. She kept up a running chatter.

"Mom said to put you in the children's wing." She spoke over her shoulder, smiling. Dean resembled his mother, but Madeleine's sexy lips were the only feature she shared with them. She wore her wavy black hair long with auburn highlights. Her round face and gray eyes glowed with mischief. Sometime since I last saw her, she'd showered and changed into jeans and a sleeveless blouse showing off her muscled arms. "That's where Dean's and my rooms are. We can all hang out after supper."

Great. Now I'd have to sleep within fifty feet of him. No doubt he'd want to argue some more before the night was over.

"Where does Lisette stay?" I tried to keep any venom out of my voice, but I knew I didn't fool Madeleine. She let out a cute, girlish giggle, reminding me of my best friend Hannah Kessler.

"Lisette goes home before dinner, thank God. But now that you're here, I don't know. She might want to stay." She made a sick face. I laughed in spite of myself.

We stopped in front of a closed door. Madeleine reached out for the doorknob but hesitated. She smiled apologetically at me and tried again, this time pushing the door open. Light flooded from the room's open blinds and spotlighted a painting on the hallway wall. Recognizing the painting's subject as the same girl I saw on the road, the one who caused me to wreck my wonderful car, I bit back a gasp. *So she belonged at this house?*

"Who is—" I began.

"Lisette is having—" Madeleine began at the same time.

"You first." We said together and laughed.

"No, really, you first," I said. "I want to hear what you have to say about Lisette. Your mom said she was raised here, but it's uncomfortable as hell."

"I bet!" Madeleine motioned me into the room. "Mom's totally hoodwinked by her, but she's a mean bitch. Don't let her catch you off guard. I was so excited when Dean said he was seeing someone from Gaslight City. I hoped he had moved on."

"So spill," I said. "What's her story?"

"Well, I don't remember her living here. By the time I got old enough to be able to remember, she and Dean were already married," Madeleine said. "She was an awful sister-in-law. She'd put on such a show when people could see her and just ignore me the rest of the time. Once, she forgot me at the Mall of Louisiana in Baton Rouge."

I gaped at her, imagining the terror she must have felt.

"Supposedly, she's come home to visit her folks because her husband is in France on business," she continued in my silence. "After Daddy got hurt and she found out Dean was coming in, she's been over here as much as she can manage. She probably wants to get back together with him." She stopped speaking and walked to the open doorway and pulled the door shut. "I overheard Daddy telling Mom her husband is being indicted for embezzling a bunch of money and is hiding in France."

Wow. Dean's family life competed with any soap opera I'd ever watched. Maybe his reasons for not introducing me had something to do with all the drama. Knowing this beautifully manicured house and its inhabitants were far from perfect made me less angry at Dean. *Maybe I need to give him a break.*

For the first time, I looked around the room. The bed featured a heavy curving brass frame, an antique by the looks of it, and a delicate eyelet comforter. A vanity table with a scalloped mirror sat against the wall opposite the two huge windows facing the lawn. I walked to the window and looked out on the grounds.

From the second floor window, the workers cleaning up the mess left by the flood looked far removed from the world inside this house. I imagined how many girls and women must have looked out this very window. Had they all been born into this family? Or had some of them been like me, an outsider who wasn't sure she belonged?

A group of workers moved on to another pile of rubbish and cleared my line of sight. The ghost girl stood looking up at the window. A cold bolt of fear worked its way through me. I had to know who she was so I could figure out how to get her to leave me alone. With all the normal couple issues between Dean and me, a close encounter of the ghost kind would only worsen the tension.

"Madeleine, the girl in the painting, the one in the hall, who is that?"

Madeleine sighed and clasped her hands in front of her. "That's my sister, Shayne. This is her room."

I forced a smile, ignoring my tight throat and thundering pulse. "I thought so."

"Mom just had the room redone to use as a guest room. Before that, well, it was locked all my life."

Madeleine had just turned twenty-one. So whatever happened to Shayne happened a very long time ago.

"Where is Shayne now?"

Madeleine jumped and glanced around the room, as though afraid she might be overheard even with the door closed. When she spoke, she did so in a loud whisper. "She disappeared before I was even born. They never figured out what became of her."

From the look of it, Shayne didn't meet a peaceful or an easy end. Dread knotted painful lumps in my tense muscles. I so didn't want to get in the middle of this family's drama. I ran my hand over the sheer lace curtains. Something clanked to the floor, and I jumped away, wondering what I'd broken, cheeks already flaming.

Madeline must've thought I broke something, too. She rushed over and stared at the object on the floor. I saw nothing more than a jumbled mess of silver with a black stone connected to it. Thinking it was a fancy pull for the blinds, I scooped it up, intent on fixing my mess. The chain spread out, and I realized I held a piece of jewelry.

The delicate chain was made up of elongated ovals, each one containing the same delicate filigree pattern. Rather than feeling cool in my hand, it felt pleasantly warm as though alive. A large, black stone pendant hung from the necklace. It reflected a kaleidoscope of color, and the colors seemed to dance when I touched the stone.

"What on earth is that thing doing up here?" Madeline wrinkled her nose and held out her hand for the piece of jewelry. Though it wasn't mine, I hated to give it up. Holding it, touching it, felt good. Reluctantly, I handed it to her. She tucked it into her jeans pocket. "This is Mom's. I can't imagine how it got up here. It belonged to my great-grandmother. She was a flapper in the jazz era." We exchanged smiles, and she motioned me to follow her, pacing her steps with mine as the hallway floorboards creaked beneath our feet. "I know old stuff like this is all the rage, but just between you and me, this thing's gaudy."

I disagreed. It was beautiful. I made a noncommittal sound.

"Plus, you know what I heard?" She leaned close, grabbing my arm for emphasis. "I heard the lady who owned it was a *witch*."

Oh great. What else could happen to make this trip worse? Turned out, I didn't have to wait long to find out.

MADELEINE RETURNED the necklace to Julienne, who nearly jumped out of her skin when she saw it. She gave me the oddest look, one which made me squirm. I asked Madeleine to take me to where Dean was. He needed to know the part Shayne's ghost played in me staying. Besides, guilt over my bad behavior had choked out my anger. Dean's lie of omission sucked, but so did the way I flew off the handle.

We found him helping the other workers clear debris. Poor Madeleine fled back to house, swatting at mosquitoes. I picked up a shovel and worked alongside him, trying to think of the right way to start a conversation. Other than a sharp nod, he didn't acknowledge me, which meant he'd just as soon I disappear.

"Who's this, Dean-o?" The speaker had a heavier build than Dean but wasn't any taller. His wide shoulders gave way to thick arms looking like they could support the weight of the world. Where Dean resembled his mother, this man resembled Madeleine with his round face and wavy black hair. I could only guess this was another sibling I'd never heard of.

Dean's jaw clenched either at the nickname or at having to mess with me so soon after our argument. He jammed his shovel into a soggy pile of branches and leaves and turned to the larger man. "Dino is the name of Fred Flintstone's pet dinosaur. How many times have I asked you not to call me that?"

"Oh, just about six million since you learned to talk."

Dean pressed his lips together and rolled his eyes. "And I still don't like it. But that's okay. I guess I can act like an adult about it." He sidled closer to me and put his arm around my waist, surprising me. "*Little Ricky*, this is Peri Jean Mace...my girlfriend. Peri Jean, this is my older brother, *Little Ricky*."

"Nice to meet you, ma'am." He held out a veined hand and flashed white, straight teeth. His good humor made me smile, and we exchanged a hard squeeze. "I gotta ask, Peri Jean, how'd a beautiful woman like you get involved with such a serious fuddy-duddy like Dean-o?"

"I'm a serious fuddy-duddy, too." I said it deadpan, and Ricky howled. Dean grunted and went back to his work.

Ricky slapped Dean on the back and got a scowl in return. He turned back to me. "Hey, Peri Jean, you gotta meet Colton Starr. He's an honorary Turgeau."

He grabbed my arm and led me away from Dean. "Colton! Hey, man, you gotta meet Dean's lady. She seems okay, even though she's cozy with the king of the sticks in the mud."

We walked up behind a man covered head to toe in black mud. The mess was worst near his feet where the gunk had caked and dried and then had more added to it. The fertile scent of the rich black soil hung in the air. The smell burrowed deep into my subconscious, awakening something I couldn't have described. This land had a pulse of its own, a magic that spoke to me. I struggled to stay focused on Ricky.

Colton turned to face us, swiping at his face with his shirt sleeve, which only smeared the mud into his blonde hair. We both widened our eyes in recognition.

"Well, hello again, pretty lady." Colton's dimples deepened into the kind of smile that could stop traffic.

"You two..." Ricky glanced between us, trying to figure out how we knew each other.

"We met when I first got here."

"Trey, drunk as a lord, accosted her in the parking area." Colton rolled his eyes.

"That loser." Ricky shook his head. "I know Mom and Dad feel guilty about what happened with Shayne, but I think they should fire him."

I perked up, hoping he'd say more about Shayne, but he was obviously finished.

"He needs work," Colton said. "No telling how badly he'd deteriorate if he was unemployed."

Ricky grunted, and Colton dropped the subject and turned to me.

"I taught Dean his senior year in high school," he said. "I hope he's learned to behave since then."

I took a closer look at Colton. He was perhaps a few years older than Ricky but not many.

"You think I'm not old enough, don't you?" Colton's face creased into an even bigger smile, and I saw a little more age around his eyes and mouth. "It was my first teaching job."

"I still think you're lying," I said. Colton's answering giggle told me I'd said the right thing. Conceited. I didn't blame him. "Do you still teach at the same school?"

"No," he said. "Luckily, I got my Ph.D. and moved to the college level. I teach at Tulane in New Orleans. When I heard Big Rick was hurt, I couldn't stay away. The Turgeaus are like the family I never had. You just wait. They'll take you under their wing, and you'll be the same way."

Thinking of my rapidly dwindling family, which consisted only of my sick grandmother, I glanced at Dean. He made a show of ignoring us. Whether I fell in love with this family, or they with me, remained to be seen. Dean's and my future played a big part in what happened. An uncomfortable silence fell over us until Ricky shrugged and began picking up debris a few feet away. Colton, his eyes flicking between Dean and me, followed after a few seconds. I walked back to Dean and got back to work.

"I'm sorry, baby." Dean spoke in such a quiet voice, I had to lean close to hear him. "I handled this wrong all the way around. You didn't deserve to be kept in the dark about my family." He reached for my hand, and I let him thread his fingers through mine, reveling in the little thrill of lust I still felt every time he touched me. His eyes held mine, waiting for me to take ownership of the hurts I'd caused him.

"I'm sorry too." Admitting my wrongdoing both stung and relieved tension. "I don't know why I can't spend the night at your house. I get restless, and I just go home. I do want to be with you, though."

Dean shrugged, leaned over, and kissed my cheek. He whispered in my ear, "Want to go dancing tonight? I'll show you the bar I used to sneak into when I was underage."

I giggled at his breath tickling my ear and nudged him away. It was time to tell him about Shayne. Dread gnawed at my guts. If I had the power to change one thing about myself, I'd make myself normal.

We'd patched up our little spat, but he sure wasn't going to like what I needed to tell him next.

5

MY ABILITY TO see ghosts shitted up my life magnificently. It made most people uncomfortable around me. It made me uncomfortable as hell too. Most of my life, I hid it. Then, six months ago, an encounter with a dark entity heightened my sensitivity to the spirit world. The spirits had even more power to infiltrate my life, and I had even less power to stop them.

I hated dragging Dean into it. He tried to understand, but he didn't quite get it. He always got this sick look on his face, and it made *me* feel sick. But he needed to know his dead sister wanted something from me. I took a deep breath and braced myself.

"Dean, I have something to tell you. Running my car into that mud bath wasn't just bad judgment. My brakes went out—"

"Yeah, they just locked up. The mechanic said he'd—"

Is he deliberately acting obtuse? Frustrated, I talked over him, even though he hated it. "Forget the brakes. I saw… something in the driveway. I swerved to miss it."

"What? An animal?" The fear in Dean's eyes gave away his lame attempt to play dumb. "I watched you drive away. I didn't see anything. Maybe the sun blinded you?"

"It wasn't the sun." I massaged my temples, trying to chase away the headache forming behind my eyes. "I think I saw Shayne."

Dean jumped as though shocked. "What do you know about Shayne?"

His gaze darted to where his brother and Colton Starr horsed around a few feet away, giggling and trying to push each other into the mud. He didn't have to say anything for me to understand. I hoped they didn't find out about me too. I'd rather streak naked across the lawn for everyone's entertainment. Less humiliation involved.

"I'm staying in her room." Anxiety distilled the world around me, isolating every sound, making the colors seem too bright and the smells unbearable. I sucked in a deep breath and tried to calm down. When I spoke again, relating all the times I'd seen Shayne, my voice held only a slight tremor.

Dean put his hand over his mouth and muttered something that sounded sort of like a prayer. He squinted at me, making me very aware of this talent I had, this thing I never wanted to do. "Can you find out what happened to her? Who hurt her?"

"I figure that's what she wants. You want me to try?" I stared into Dean's eyes. He never asked me to use my ability.

"No." He grabbed his shovel and jammed it into the soft earth, burying the metal part completely. "Yes." He shook his head and shrugged. "I don't know."

"I hate being the one to tell you she's passed on."

"Don't be. In my heart, I knew." He jerked the shovel out of the dirt, lifted a pile of debris, and hefted it into the wheelbarrow. This side of him was so like me, desperate for something to do when things got uncomfortable. When he spoke, his voice trembled. "You ever heard of Marcus Lewis?"

I shook my head.

"Marcus Lewis was a serial killer who got caught in California. The press called him The Tennis Coach."

"Ahh, yeah," I said. "I think I've seen a TV documentary about him." Lewis had taught tennis anywhere he could—health clubs, country clubs, private lessons. He picked his victims from his students. He was convicted of only two murders, but the documentary hinted law enforcement believed there were more. Many more.

"Soon as the news broke about his arrest, and his picture flashed on the TV screen, I recognized him. He used to teach tennis at the country club where our family had a membership."

"Oh God, Dean." My lame words did little to express how terrible I felt for him.

"I pulled every string I had, both in law enforcement and with my family's influence, and got one of the investigating officers to speak to him about Shayne." Dean worked with his back to me, lost in his horrifying memories. "The investigator told me Lewis wouldn't admit to anything, but he was able to describe a scar on Shayne's hip. It was a scar he couldn't have seen unless he saw her naked."

Dean's story crawled over my skin, making me shiver. I approached him and put my hand on his sweat-dampened back because I didn't know what else to do. Other than a slight jerk when I touched him, he didn't respond but kept talking.

"Lewis wouldn't give them any real information. He wanted a deal, immunity for any cases he helped close and the possibility of parole, and nobody was willing to make that deal with him." His voice hitched, and he stopped digging and leaned on the shovel. "Everybody looked for Shayne's body again, thinking she might have been Lewis's first victim, but they never found her."

He turned to me, his eyes brimming with tears. "I try to find solace in Lewis rotting in prison. But I don't."

I moved closer and put my arm around him. He leaned into me and laid his head on my shoulder. I trailed my fingers along the back of his neck.

"Earlier, you wanted to know why I never talk about these people." He cut his eyes in the direction the big house. "About this place. It's because of Shayne. I was a senior in high school and she was a junior when she disappeared. I was the last person who talked to her. Maybe I could have saved her. But I didn't." Standing slouched with his hands shoved in his pockets, Dean looked desolate and alone. "Ricky was away at college, already a junior. It upset him, sure, but he didn't have to be here for the fallout."

"I can't begin to imagine. I guess Madeleine came along when Shayne never came back."

Dean huffed an angry laugh and wiped his face. "Mom got pregnant the summer after I graduated high school. Madeleine was her replacement daughter. I always figured she just wanted to forget."

I shrugged, not wanting to agree or disagree. Dean had a right to his feelings on the matter. I suspected he felt like an outsider as his parents tried to rebuild their lives. In the absence of my parents, my grandmother was always there for me. I wondered who had been there for Dean. Lisette? *Zoiks.*

"If you want me to figure out who killed Shayne, I'll do my best." I left out the part where it would take communicating with the dead to do it.

Dean put his arm around me and sighed. He was quiet for a long time. "I never thought I'd say this. Please. Put it to rest for me."

"Then I'll have to know some things about her." When I solved my cousin's murder six months ago, I learned things about her I never wanted to know. I wondered if it would be the same with Shayne.

Dean shivered and stared into the distance. My heart ached. He might love me, but this part of me made him uncomfortable. I knew just how he felt. About the time he got ready to say something, we both spotted Ricky walking toward us holding shingles in both hands. I looked back at the big house, searching for the source of the damage.

He understood and said, "There's some old shacks behind those trees. Storm demolished one of 'em. Needed to be torn down anyway. That's a mess I don't look forward to facing."

"Where's Colton?" Dean asked.

"Driving Mom and Maddy to the hospital to visit Daddy. You know Daddy likes Colton more than he ever liked us."

Dean grunted. Ricky turned his attention to me. "You doing all right out here? My wife sure wouldn't want to do this kind of work. My sons either, for that matter."

"My nephews are eight and thirteen and allergic to work." Dean shoved another pile of debris into his wheelbarrow. Ricky snorted and started the first of many stories about his two sons, who sounded like a handful.

I listened with only half an ear. My nicotine monkey danced around my mind screaming for me to feed it. As soon as it seemed polite, I wandered away from the two men, intent on taking a smoke break. Some force pulled me toward the old shacks, and I went, halfway scared of what waited for me back there. But I promised to help, and I would. I took a wheelbarrow to make it look legit.

WALKING toward the screen of trees, I kept my steps light, knowing the thick mud could have a quicksand effect. I dug my cigarettes out of my pocket and jammed one into my mouth and lit it. Cigarette dangling from my lips, I picked up a few more branches and tossed them into the wheelbarrow.

As I walked deeper into the trees, the soupy air settled

over me, heavy and dense. I felt sweat dampen my skin to the point of slickness. Mosquitoes hummed around my head, competing for attention with my racing thoughts about Dean and his dead sister. His desire for me to use my ability to solve her murder surprised me and made me skeptical. Was he trying to decide if he could live with this part of me? Or was this an act of desperation?

If I were one of those girls who'd had three or four really serious boyfriends instead of enough flings to fill a —well, let's not go there—I'd know what it meant in terms of our relationship. But I was dumbfounded, worried this would open a can of something I didn't even want to think about. I halfway wanted to talk it out with another female, but who?

My only female friend, Hannah Kessler, was vacationing in the Cook Islands in Rarotonga at a beach house she won in her divorce. If I called, she'd want me to drop everything and fly out there. *Pass.*

My grandmother might have advice, but the involvement of Shayne's ghost would disturb her. Though Memaw didn't have it, my weird talent ran in our family. She would worry until I came home. A woman dying of cancer had better things to do than fret over me.

I was on my own for this rodeo. Scared didn't begin to describe my feelings. Since my abilities had intensified, I really didn't know what Shayne could do to me. And this was murder. Murderers tended to get pissed when someone blew the whistle on them. If someone other than the serial killer Dean mentioned had killed Shayne, which I thought likely, they'd gotten away with murder for a mighty long time. Getting caught now could end ugly.

But, in the deepest part of my heart, I wanted to fix this for Dean. Well, not fix it. But make it bearable. I owed him that much for storming down here clutching that receipt like the star of a romantic comedy.

The row of run-down shacks appeared in front of me, nearly overgrown with wild saplings. The gray, unpainted wood gave them a spooky look. I noticed new padlocks on their doors and bars on the first two buildings.

The other three buildings had simply rotted in the soupy South Louisiana air. The glass in one of the windows had broken, leaving a gaping black hole. I took a step backward from the sight, thinking of the slaves who lived here at one time. I felt them, their sad, lost energy reaching out to me. A hiss of whispers rose up from the ground, and I hurried away.

Cold fingers closed around my arm, and my nerves did a quick jump. I bit back a scream. After all, I'd come looking for Shayne. Of course she found me.

I stubbed out my cigarette, ignoring my swimming head, and faced Shayne. She'd been a pretty girl. Of course, her gray lips and the black holes where her eyes had been chilled me. The sound of whispers filled my head. Nothing intelligible. Just a bunch of talking all at once.

"Who did it, Shayne?" Prior to six months ago, I never talked to any ghost. But after my sensitivities increased, I sometimes understood a word within the whispers if I asked the right question.

Shayne motioned me to follow. She flitted in and out of my vision, moving lightning fast, leading me through a small copse of trees. I picked my way after her, very mindful of the copperheads, timber rattlers, water moccasins, and coral snakes that lived in the area. It was just warm enough for them to stir after hibernating for winter. They couldn't hurt Shayne, but they might kill me. Especially so far from a hospital.

Shayne waited for me next to the final building, which the recent flood unseated from its foundations and turned into a pile of rubble. She stood where the floor would have been. I heard the sound of a shovel digging into the earth. I looked around the area, expecting to see someone with us, before realizing Shayne was making me hear the shovel. My breath came in shaking gasps as the heebie-jeebies took over, but I forced myself to remain receptive to Shayne. I wanted to get this done.

It only took a second to see what she wanted me to see. The bone of a skull, filthy, winked at me from the fertile earth. I slumped, remembering the sound of a shovel hitting and disturbing soil. Someone buried her. Maybe alive. Wild horror forced its way through me, and a wave of dizziness rocked me on my feet.

"All right, then. Let me call your brother and see what we can do." I used my cell phone to call Dean, pushing the buttons with shaking fingers. When he picked up, I had to clear my throat to speak. "I've found your sister's remains by the old shacks."

"How do you know it's her?"

"She led me to it."

I hung up on his sharp intake of breath and sat down on one of the piers on which the house had sat. I saw the rest of the body, just visible beneath some shallow dirt. Something silver winked at me from the makeshift grave. Poor Shayne. I tried to piece this burial location together with her walking alongside the road beat-up, and my throat tightened. Had she gone out for a walk and gotten attacked by the kind of man who hurts women? Or did someone she knew do this to her?

"Shayne, who did this?" I looked around for my ghostly guide, but she was gone. Maybe this was all she wanted. I knew that was almost as likely as a pig learning to talk. A girl could hope, though.

The shouts and bustle of Dean and the other workmen approaching reached me. As they broke into the clearing, I waved Dean over. The sadness in his eyes hurt me to the depths of my soul.

6

———

A DARK CLOUD rolled over the sky and a clap of thunder boomed somewhere nearby. A few members of the Saint Namadie Parish Sheriff's Office jumped and glanced in the direction of the thunder.

"Shit," Dean yelled. "Gonna rain again, and we're trying to get my dead sister out of the mud."

"Mr. Turgeau, the East Baton Rouge Parish Medical Examiner came all the way over here to St. Namadie Parish as a favor to my office. They're the best in the state, and *we* are doing the best we can." The gray-haired man I pegged as sheriff spoke in a conciliatory tone. "We want to see what happened to this person, and it may not even be your sister."

"It is." Dean's voice rose even more. "See that silver in the dirt? She had a pin in her hip."

Ricky went to his brother's side, grabbed his arm, and dragged him away from the sheriff, whispering in his ear. Dean jerked away and came to stand near me. A muscle in his jaw jumped every few seconds, and a vein throbbed at his temple. I could tell he was close to having a breakdown of some sort and wanted to comfort him, but knew it wouldn't help. I tensed my muscles in preparation for having to help drag Dean away from the crime scene. Ricky tried touching his younger brother's shoulder. Dean's arm flashed out, slapping his hand away. The stocky man came to stand on the other side of me.

"Did you call Colton?" Dean asked across me. "Didn't you say he's at the hospital with Mom and Dad?"

"Not yet. They don't have any way of knowing it's her," Ricky said. I pressed my lips together and shrugged. Unless Shayne was playing an elaborate prank, I knew for a fact these were her remains. I opened my mouth to tell Ricky but bit back my words. He might not want to know what I knew. And how Dean would react to me telling him was anybody's guess. So I said nothing, although remaining quiet made me squirm.

"Call him," Dean said louder than necessary. A few uniforms from the crime scene glanced our way.

The sheriff walked to our little group, his lips and eyes pinched with tension. "Folks, the ME has asked that all non-law enforcement vacate the premises." Dean opened his mouth to protest, but the sheriff cut him off. "Being in law enforcement yourself, I know you understand."

Dean flushed. Knowing him like I did, I figured he'd been ready to use his career as a way to remain on the scene. He needed to get out of here before he really lost it. I took his hand in mine.

"Come on. You can help her more if you're somewhere else."

Dean grabbed my hand and squeezed, grinding the bones together. I gritted my teeth at the pain but refused to pull away when he needed me. He leaned close and whispered in my ear so Ricky wouldn't hear what he had to say. "You're still going to see if you can figure out who killed her, right?"

Talk about a role reversal. This was the first time Dean ever admitted to needing my help. I hoped I didn't let him down. "If she'll help me," I spoke just above a whisper. "I haven't seen her since I found the bones. It may be all she wanted."

Dean took off walking without an answer, pulling me along behind him. Ricky followed us, taking out his phone and placing a call to Colton. He spoke quickly, obviously leaving a voicemail, and jogged to catch up to us. The three of us walked back to the house without talking. Once there, Dean reminded us Julienne wouldn't want her house dirtied, so we sat in a flower-filled brick courtyard on wrought-iron furniture.

"You saw the pin, huh?" Tears rolled down Ricky's face, and his mouth twisted as he tried not to cry in front of me. I turned my back to him so he wouldn't feel embarrassed. Behind me, he wept.

"What was the pin from?" I needed to make noise so I could pretend not to hear Ricky crying.

"Our mother had a car wreck when Shayne was a little girl. She had to have a pin in her hip." Dean spoke to me as though Ricky wasn't crying. "And yes, I saw it."

"I can't believe it's her. Not after all these years." Ricky choked out the words and put his hands over his face. Dean and I squirmed in our chairs. When the other man's sobs slowed, Dean handed him a white cloth handkerchief. Ricky wiped his face, then stared at the barn.

"I ought to go out there now and beat the truth out of that pathetic runt myself." Ricky's body was tense. He jabbed an accusing finger in the direction of the barn. "If we want to know what happened to Shayne, that's where the answers are."

I raised my eyebrows at Dean in question. He sighed and shook his head.

"Trey and Shayne dated before she disappeared. They actually broke up a few months before she went missing. Something went on between them, and Shayne was afraid of him."

"Tell you what that something was, little brother." Ricky leaned forward, resting his thick forearms on the table. "I was home from college that weekend. Shayne was doing those interviews. Remember that?"

Dean listened intently, his eyes on his brother's face. I made a mental note to ask him about the interviews later. If Shayne was dealing with a lot of different people, one of them might have hurt her.

"She came driving up in that old junky station wagon Mom gave her, all red-faced and upset. She was shaking so hard she could barely get her things out of the car." Ricky leaned back in his chair, fury simmering in his eyes. "I asked her what was wrong, and she said she and Trey got into an argument. Wouldn't tell me over what. But, Dean-o, she had these scratches on her arm, looked like some kinda animal made them."

"Why didn't you ever tell anybody?" Dean frowned at his older brother.

"Because...I...went to see him." Ricky's shoulders rounded.

"You kicked his ass?" I clarified. He shrugged and would not meet my gaze. So jovial Ricky had a temper.

"The sheriff investigated Trey, but said he was clean," Dean said to me. "Mom and Dad felt guilty for suspecting him and insisted he stay on."

I glanced at the barn and considered Trey as the one who killed Shayne. Despite what Dean said about the investigation turning up nothing, I had no trouble seeing him as her murderer. His instability struck me as a lifelong affliction. Their failed romance added in motive. Next time I saw Shayne's ghost, I'd try to direct her to communicating with me about Trey.

"Shit." Dean's yell made me jump. "That's Lisette's car pulling up to the house. Who the hell called her?" He glared at Ricky.

"Not me." Ricky's wide eyes could have been elaborate acting or the real deal. "Mom may have. You know she still considers her family."

Julienne's Jaguar sedan appeared not far behind Lisette's Mercedes. Upon seeing their mother's car, both brothers rose. Dean held out a hand to pull me up. I took it not because I needed it but because I liked the gesture and hoped Lisette was watching. The three of us walked toward Julienne's car, me trailing a little behind and feeling like the worst kind of intruder. I noticed Lisette sat in her car an extra few seconds, applying makeup. I shook my head.

The story Dean told me about his divorce involved infidelity and a lot of hurt feelings. I didn't understand why Julienne still considered someone who cheated on her son as family, regardless of whether Lisette grew up with the Turgeau children.

Dean and Ricky reached their mother. The older woman cried openly, clutching both her sons and Madeleine to her. Colton put his arms around the weeping family and leaned his head against Julienne's. I kept my distance, feeling my otherness more than ever. This was not my family.

Lisette, on the other hand, did no such thing. She threw herself into the circle of mourners, slipping under Dean's arm. He pulled away as if burned and walked toward me.

"Come on," he said. "No doubt you'll want to shower before dinner. I'll get you some towels and show you the bathroom."

Though Madeleine had already done those things, I followed him silently.

FRESHLY SHOWERED, I sat in Madeleine's pink nightmare of a room while she rifled through her closet to find me a dress for dinner. I had no idea people in the twenty-first century still dressed for dinner.

"I can't believe your mother is cooking dinner."

"That's Mom." She sat down on an overstuffed fuchsia chair. "Her words were, 'They'll find what they find, and we'll deal with it then. For right now, we'll keep things as normal as possible.'" While speaking Julienne's words, Madeleine sat ramrod straight and used her mother's overly proper way of speaking. I bit back a smile. She was a good actress. "Fuck steel magnolias," she said. "That's not what a southern belle is. Mom is a true southern belle. She looks as delicate as lace, but she's pure cast iron and bailing wire."

I liked Madeleine. She wasn't as intense as Dean, but she had his focus and confidence. If I had more family, I'd want someone like her in it.

"I heard Ricky say you found her." Her eyes rested on me.

"There are—were, I guess—some shacks past the barn—"

"That's what's left of the slave quarters." She bit her lip. "We like to pretend that period in history didn't happen..."

"But it did," I said, wondering if that was why brush and trees had been allowed to grow between the big house and the old slaves' quarters. *Easier to live next to horror if you couldn't see it.*

"Yep." Madeleine played with a t-shirt, folding it, shaking it out, and refolding it. "Shayne was a skeleton?" She squirmed.

I nodded. "Have you ever heard anybody speculate on who might have hurt her?"

"I wasn't even born when she disappeared. By the time

I was old enough to be aware, no one ever talked about it. One time, Daddy'd been drinking at Christmas and he got into an argument with Mom, saying if they'd never let Shayne drive all over the county interviewing people, nothing would have happened to her."

Those interviews again. Now was my chance to find out more. "Interviews?"

"Yeah. Shayne and Colton put together these books about the Cajun culture. I don't know much about them, but if Colton comes to dinner, he'll talk your ear off about them."

That didn't tell me much, but I'd talk to Colton as soon as I could.

"How is your father?" I wondered if he'd insist on coming home from the hospital to oversee these newest developments.

"Horrible. Mean. Contrary."

I glanced at Madeleine for elaboration, but she offered none. Instead she stared into the deepening gloom outside her window. When she spoke, her voice had lost its jaunty edge. "Do you think someone killed her back there?"

"Maybe." The two of us stared at each other a long moment. Then Madeleine presented me with a cocktail dress to wear to dinner and a pair of uncomfortable shoes to go with it. Horrors on top of horrors. She insisted I try it on. Though she had a more stocky, muscular build than I, it fit perfectly. I wanted to cry.

After taking as long as I possibly could to dress, I found myself limping after her, feeling like a circus clown, dreading pre-dinner drinks in the library.

7

———

MADELEINE STOPPED OUTSIDE THE LIBRARY, her hand on the knob. "In case I don't get a chance to tell you: one thing you ought to know about Mom's cooking...it's bad. She's good at everything else, but she can't cook to save her life. Try not to let it show on your face."

Without waiting for my answer, she opened the door and motioned me to enter ahead of her. I slunk into the room, stiff with discomfort.

Not only did Madeleine's borrowed dress itch, the short skirt flared out, threatening to show my panties. It plunged deep into my cleavage and revealed a tattoo I usually keep hidden, one which caused Madeleine's eyes to widen when she saw it. I almost groaned when I saw Colton Starr standing in front of the bookshelves holding a drink.

"Hey, girl." He sauntered over to me, confident in his soft gray linen suit. His green-flecked tie set off his eyes. Despite the gloomy day, a riotous sunset streamed through the windows, playing on the blond highlights in his hair. He was magnificently hot. I, on the other hand, felt like a chihuahua in a ball gown.

I bet none of these people can figure out what Dean is doing with me. I tried to ignore the sinking feeling in my stomach.

Ricky stood from a corner chair. I hadn't seen him in the shadows. He wore a jacket and slacks with an open necked shirt. "Love that dress. Looks a lot better on you than it does on the squirt." He tipped his chin at Madeleine who crossed her eyes and stuck out her tongue.

Sipping club soda with lime, I wandered around the library, reading the spines of the endless books. The Turgeaus observed no filing system that I could figure. Books on Louisiana history sat next to the kind of romance novels Memaw liked to read. I even saw a section of zombie books. I stopped in front of a glassed-in display featuring a picture of Shayne, the invisible guest of honor. The books all bore the same title, *Cajuns: The Disappearing Culture.* A closer look revealed a different volume number on each book. There were six volumes in all, each with Colton Starr's name prominently listed below the title. Underneath his name, in very small print, was "with the help of the St. Namadie Parish High School's History Club."

These had to be the books Madeleine mentioned upstairs. Inside the display sat a framed newspaper article awarding Shayne a posthumous humanitarian award and an honorary degree in anthropology from Tulane University. A face appeared next to my reflection in the glass.

Immediately recognizing Shayne's messy cloud of dark hair and the streak of dirt on her cheek, I sucked in my breath and held very still.

Shayne turned to me, as though she wanted to whisper in my ear. Icy air burned the tender skin, and I heard a muffled noise. It could have been a word or a moan. *Please, please, please don't let them start talking to me.* The idea sent ice through my veins.

"It was her pet project," a voice behind me said. I jumped and let out a yelp. Colton Starr took my arm. "I'm sorry, hon. Are you okay?"

"I'm sorry." I thought fast and made up an excuse. "I was so engrossed in this I wasn't paying attention. Madeleine mentioned these." I faced Colton and forced a smile, ignoring my thudding heart. "I'm staying in Shayne's room."

"Julienne told me she was renovating the room for guests. After today's horrible events, I'm sure you're curious about her."

"And these books. Dean has mentioned them too."

"This is hard for him." Colton nodded, his mouth set in a grim line. "He and Shayne were close. Irish twins, you know?"

I didn't. "Irish twins?"

"Sorry. I probably wouldn't know the term had it not been applied to my sister and me." He gave me that killer smile. "The term, which is very old, means siblings born within a year of each other. Dean and Shayne were eleven months apart, if memory serves. The timing of their birthdays put them in separate grades, but they were thick. Almost like real twins. He took her loss personally."

Sounded like Dean. Our months together had taught me he took most everything personally. *Takes one to know one.*

"So what about these books? I was told you worked on them with Shayne."

"The project was Shayne's idea. She was very interested in this community and its history. This area has been settled a very long time." Colton went around to the back of the case, opened it, and took out one of the books. He handed it to me. "She envisioned a series of books that illuminated Cajun culture the way *Foxfire* books captured Appalachian culture."

I opened the book and flipped through, stopping at pictures of elderly people showing off crafts and tools their ancestors used.

"I helped her apply for grants, got her to sit in while I conducted the field research, and showed her how to sift through the interviews."

An invisible force slammed the book from my hands. I jumped and fumbled the book, which rocketed to the floor near my feet. Embarrassment and irritation heated my body, and a bead of sweat ran down my side. *Why do ghosts have to be so forceful?* The last thing I wanted was Colton knowing my dirty little secret.

"After teaching for so many years, I realize teachers only get students like her once or twice over the course of a career." Colton bent to pick up the book, using the movement to cover wiping away a tear. He straightened and tried to smile at me. "Myself, I would not be where I am now without having worked on this project. Her loss haunts me every day."

I scrambled for a way to talk about this without making Colton break down. Of course this upset him. He taught Shayne, saw her every day. But she reacted when he mentioned interviews. I needed to find out more about those.

The door opened, cutting off my mad brainstorm of questions to ask about the interviews. Dean walked into the library. Before that moment, I never realized men could sparkle. But he did. From his clean shaven face to the tips of his shiny black shoes, he personified hot dude in a suit. I caught Colton's amused gaze and realized my mouth hung open. I closed it with a pop.

"I came in to tell y'all dinner's ready." He crossed the room and kissed my cheek. "And, Peri Jean, just so you know, my mother's talent is not cooking. Try to keep your expression neutral as you eat."

Colton chuckled. "Even so, Julienne's dinners are grand affairs."

"Madeleine told me, but thanks for the warning." I took his arm—first time in my life I'd ever done that—and turned toward the door. As I took the first step, something heavy slid off my foot and clattered to the floor. I gasped, thinking one of the hideous rhinestones had fallen off Madeleine's obviously pricey shoes, and looked down.

On the floor lay that necklace from upstairs. *Where the hell did that come from?* Dean, following my gaze, blanched and swooped down to pick it up. The iridescent veins of color now pulsed and writhed in the globe, reflecting off its base of delicate silver leaves. Again, I was struck by the piece's unusual beauty. Dean seemed quite shaken. He stared at the pendant, then gave me a long, hard look.

Julienne appeared at the door. "Aren't y'all hungry for some of my bouillabaisse?" Her eyes tracked to the necklace in Dean's hand, and her mouth dropped open. "Heavens. Did I set this down in here?"

But she hadn't. When Madeleine gave it to her earlier, she'd taken it into her bedroom.

"I think I may have stepped on it. It was on the floor." I couldn't quite bring myself to admit it had been on top of my foot and fell off when I took a step because there was no way in the world to explain how it got there.

Julienne stared at me for a long moment, her eyes widening. She recovered quickly and took the necklace from Dean. To me, she said, "That's quite all right, dear. I thought about wearing it to the hospital and then changed my mind. I wondered where I left it when I took it off." She tittered and motioned us to follow her out of the room.

I went willingly enough, but I couldn't stop the questions and speculation from forming and stampeding through my mind.

Julienne was lying about planning to wear that necklace to the hospital. I knew because she lied about as well as I did. Might as well have had a neon sign over her head announcing the fact.

I glanced at Dean, trying to get a read on the situation, but he kept his eyes straight ahead. Colton, obviously just as confused as I was, craned to see the necklace Julienne held cupped in one hand, slightly away from her body.

As we passed the front door, the doorbell sounded. Julienne checked the peephole and opened the door.

Lisette, her eyes red from crying, held out a bottle of wine. "Hope I'm in time for dinner. I wanted to be with my second family tonight."

Next to me, Dean stiffened, his hand sliding to the small of my back. We exchanged a glance. *Some days it rains shit.*

A few minutes later, I sat at a mile-long dining table, my elbow brushing Dean's. The chandelier bathed us in a golden glow from another century and cast long shadows in the room's corners. The double candelabra in the table's center pushed the velvet light into motion, dancing it over our faces and the tasteless food on our plates.

Dean and his siblings didn't lie about Julienne's cooking. Dean, who usually ate like a starving man, picked at his soup and finally set down his spoon. Lisette ignored her food and proceeded to fill the air with endless banter, mostly about her husband.

The couple owned a jet, five homes in America, and a condo in Paris. Colton and Julienne asked polite questions at the proper intervals. Dean rolled his eyes when our gazes met. I itched with the desire to ask about the embezzlement charges against Carter. To my credit, I did not.

"I'm not doing this." Ricky's spoon clanked to the table.

Every eye in the room fastened on him. "I can't just sit here and act like we didn't find Shayne's body this afternoon."

"I, for one, hope they arrest Trey this time." Lisette didn't miss a beat.

"Same here." Ricky nodded. Julienne started to speak, but Ricky cut her off. "Even if he didn't do it, he knows more than he told last time. I guarantee it."

"You don't know that," Dean said. "Talk like that is exactly what gets people to take matters into their own hands. Trey was fully investigated twenty years ago."

"Did you ever get access to the case files?" Lisette's flashing eyes met Dean's across the table. Judging by the malice in her voice and the sudden stiffness in Dean's face, she knew the answer to her question.

"I don't need them." Dean narrowed his eyes at Lisette. "Watching true crime documentaries on TV doesn't make you a detective. Butt out."

"Dean Zachary Turgeau!" Julienne slapped her hand down on the table. "You will not speak that way at the dinner table."

Zachary? Ricky and I exchanged a glance, and he covered his mouth.

"And, Richard Junior, we will not discuss your poor sister at dinnertime."

I kept my eyes on my lap, not wanting Julienne to scold me.

"I've been wondering..." The sing-song innocence in Lisette's voice alerted me even as her obsidian eyes settled on me. Something about her bearing transported me back to the torture of my school days. "Exactly what do you do for a living, Peri Jean, that allows you to traipse off in the middle of the week to deliver your boyfriend's wallet?"

Her tone pissed me off. I took a deep breath and counted to ten before answering.

"I have my own business," I said in my confident businesswoman voice. "I did have to cancel some appointments, but I wanted to do this for Dean."

Lisette's lips curved into what a casual observer might have mistaken for a smile. She didn't fool me. I've tangled with the best of 'em, and she had nothing on my late cousin Rae. Still, I could tell Lisette had a hell of a zinger up her sleeve, and she intended to enjoy delivering it.

"Does this business give you the opportunity to use your psychic abilities?" She might as well have made air quotes when she said "business." Julienne coughed and took a drink of water. Lisette preened.

I stiffened as the familiar feeling of panic swelled in my throat. I had no idea how Lisette found out about me over the course of an afternoon, but she had. I glanced over at Dean and found him looking as mortified as I felt. He patted my leg under the table, his hand lingering too long on my bare thigh. Dean's mother wiped her mouth with a napkin and stared at me, her wide eyes boring into me.

"What exactly is it that you do, dear?" Though I expected surprise or maybe disgust, her words sounded nothing more than interested. Maybe a little too interested.

Lisette sat back in her chair, twirling her unused fork between her long elegant fingers, that small curve of her lips still in place. *Bitch.* I forced a smile onto my face and turned my attention to Dean's mother.

"I have an odd jobs business. People hire me for day labor doing whatever they need done." Playing clueless was the only way I knew to plug the dam. I knew it wouldn't be enough. Somehow Lisette knew about me seeing ghosts, and she would ride that horse until it hollered for mercy.

Julienne's brow wrinkled, and she tilted her head to one side. No doubt she wanted to ask what Lisette meant. I wanted to tell her she wouldn't have to wait long. This sort of cluster fuck usually played out the same way.

"So none of the odd jobs include contacting the dead?" Lisette widened her eyes dramatically and waggled her fingers. "I mean, after all your success in solving your cousin's murder—"

Dean dropped his fork with a loud clatter. His mother jumped.

"That's enough," Dean said. "Let's change the subject." A muscle in his jaw twitched, and a livid vein throbbed in his neck.

"Yes, let's do." Madeleine shot Lisette the evil eye. "Is there any dessert?"

Julienne glanced at Madeleine's nearly untouched soup and raised her eyebrows. "There isn't for you."

The tension in the room eased noticeably. Dinner ended with Julienne giving each person a job to do. She assigned Dean and Ricky to dishwashing duties. A few minutes later, their loud teasing and arguing drifted in from the kitchen. Colton took the linens to the laundry room. We girls cleared the table, making numerous trips back and forth to the kitchen, which looked like something off a glamorous TV show.

Lisette waited to strike until Julienne and Madeleine were gone from the room, and I was bent over the table brushing Ricky's cracker crumbs into a pile.

"He doesn't love you." She stood behind me and hissed the words at my back. *Cowardly twit.* I turned to face her, not even attempting to keep the fury off my face. Rather than backing away, as I'd expected, she smirked. "I can't believe Dean would sully himself with such common trash. Once he has enough of the sex, which I'll admit is probably good with someone like you, he'll move on. Plus, you're a freak. And Dean hates freaks."

My skin smoldered as embarrassment dug in its filthy claws. But a lifetime of putting up with this kind of shit brought the right words to my lips. "Obviously, he hates cheating whores too. Have you seen the way he looks at you?"

Lisette gasped and drew back her open hand.

"Do it," I said through clenched teeth. "I'll jump on you and snatch all that gorgeous hair off your head and shove it up your ass."

Tears sprang into Lisette's eyes, probably her secret weapon. Well, they wouldn't work on me. Not when she started this.

Voices, Julienne giggling and Madeleine talking, came from outside the room. Lisette jumped away from me so fast I almost didn't see her move. She manufactured a smile so genuine even I had trouble believing the last few moments really happened. As the other two women stepped into the room, she cut her eyes at me. The malice there was unmistakable. It wasn't over. Not by a long shot.

I barely listened as Lisette said her goodbyes, exchanging a tearful hug with Julienne and giving Madeleine a sisterly pat on the shoulder. I had to give Lisette her props. She missed her calling in Hollywood. Or on reality TV.

Dean's mother's cool hand closed around my arm, and she pulled me close to her. "I think we should talk privately."

When I tried to meet her eyes, she kept her gaze trained on my neck. Unable to help myself, I reached up to touch the spot she stared at. My fingers met warm metal and stone. That damn necklace again. How did the sonofabitch get there?

Fuckity fuck. Now in addition to everything else, Dean's mother would likely accuse me of theft. And I didn't know how to convince her it wasn't true.

8

———

CLIMBING the curving staircase reminded me of the walk to the principal's office after I got into yet another scuffle. I looked for signs of anger in Julienne but saw none. She climbed, her elegant hand trailing over the smooth, shining wood of the banister, as though the world simply waited on her next command. Her calm confidence reminded me of my grandmother's, and that brought to mind her cancer and how much I'd miss her when it took her. I tried to swallow around the lump forming in my throat. We walked wordlessly with only the whispers of our footsteps to mark our passage until we reached a closed double door at the end of a wing I'd have never found on my own. Julienne held the door open and motioned me inside.

Despite not wanting to draw her amusement, I did a slow circle, gaping at the room's opulence. I had stepped into an antique store where nothing was for sale.

Julienne watched me taking in everything. "This suite of rooms belonged to my grandmother, Fayette. I grew up in a different part of the house. By the time Fayette died, my own mother was confined to a hospital bed in the wing where she spent most of her married life. It seemed cruel to uproot her at that point. So Rick and I moved into this suite."

"You kept Fayette's furniture." I recognized several Art Deco pieces.

"Some." Julienne nodded. "Other pieces pre-date Fayette's residence." She motioned me into the bedroom where the furniture should have had its own historical marker and strolled to a painting near the room's center and gestured at it. "This is my grandmother, Fayette. I suspect my daughter told you she was a witch. She loves telling people that."

Julienne watched my face as I took in the painting. It portrayed Fayette as a young flapper with a bob. She posed with a small white dog. The artist had put almost human intelligence into the dog's eyes. Fayette crossed her arms across her chest and held something in her hand. I leaned closer and saw the necklace, the same one I'd encountered twice already that day. The one still hanging around my neck. I reached up and removed it and held it out to Julienne.

"Julienne, I don't know how this necklace—"

"Don't worry about that. It's no fault of yours." She accepted the necklace, walked away from the painting, and gestured for me to follow. "Fayette told me black opal has magical properties. Tons of folklore exists about the stone. Supposedly it can do some amazing things."

A million questions raced through my mind. My connection with the spirit world came from my grandmother's family. And she didn't want to discuss it. Julienne spoke about this necklace and Fayette's ability like both were just facts of life, nothing to be uncomfortable about. Julienne tilted her head as she watched me think.

"Come. Let's have this conversation in my dressing room."

We sat like proper ladies on stiff antique chairs. Julienne produced two bottled waters out of a carefully concealed mini refrigerator and made a great ceremony of emptying them into an etched crystal decanter and pouring us each a small glass. I sipped mine more out of nerves than thirst and studied Julienne's blue eyes, so like Dean's.

"I'd first like to thank you for finding Shayne and giving my family this chance at closure. We can now bury her remains in our family cemetery." She set her glass, fogged with condensation, on a matching coaster and leaned back in her chair. Her lips trembled, but she pulled herself straighter and took a deep breath. She smiled, but tears brimmed in her eyes. "This is hard. Harder than I thought it would be. About what Lisette said at supper..."

"I'm not a kook. Really." Desperation laced my words. I spent so much of life explaining this to people.

"No. You're not. Otherwise, Fayette's necklace wouldn't keep finding you."

"Was Fayette a witch?" I clapped my hand over my

mouth. The question had been too direct. Memaw would have given me a swat and told me to mind my manners.

Smile growing on her face, Julienne waved off my embarrassment. "Despite what Madeleine believes, my grandmother was not a witch." She chuckled. "But she was different from regular people. She knew things without having to be told. She had a gift, was special, like you."

Special? Odd word to describe what I am. Another lump formed in my throat. This one from gratitude. She leaned forward and squeezed my forearm. We didn't need words.

"Now I must ask you a favor, child."

I knew what was coming next, and Julienne didn't surprise me.

"I want you to use your gift to find my daughter's murderer. Rick and I are not yet old, but we soon will be. I'd like to enjoy this last chapter of my life without this *issue* hanging over our heads."

I opened my mouth to tell her Dean had already asked the same thing. She held up her hand to stop my words.

"I've been Dean's mother for nearly forty years, and I'd be a fool not to think he already set you on the same path. But I might have some information nobody else can give you."

I waited with bated breath to hear what she had to tell me. Maybe it would help. Whatever happened to Shayne haunted me more than her ghost ever could. I wanted to help this family find peace.

"The night before Shayne died, I overheard her end of a telephone conversation. She said, 'I won't let you treat me like this.' She said more but was crying. I couldn't make it out." Julienne gazed into the past, frowning, long after she quit speaking.

If Shayne threatened someone right before she disappeared, I had to find out who. But how did I do that twenty years after her murder? I'd have to have her ghost's help.

On cue, a cold chill danced over my skin. I glanced at a floor length mirror and saw Shayne standing behind her mother's chair. She raised her head, the dark holes where her eyes had been boring into me. I gasped, and Julienne twisted in her seat to see what had startled me. I dropped my gaze to my lap.

"I've never told anybody other than Sheriff Braezeale about overhearing that," she said. "But now I'm telling you because I think you'll be the one to solve Shayne's murder. Not the sheriff. He's a good man, but he's no detective, and neither is anybody who works for him."

Julienne's mouth twisted, and she turned away from me, her hand trembling as she tried to control herself. I tried to imagine what it must be like to keep moving forward after losing a child and couldn't. When she turned back, a few tear tracks marred her perfect makeup.

"If I were a detective, I'd ask you to tell me about Shayne, about her enemies, about who you think may have killed her." When Julienne said nothing, I tried a different tactic. "Ricky told me Trey—the guy who works with the horses—was a suspect."

She nodded. "Their relationship ended badly, and Shayne feared him afterward. She asked us to sell her horse." Julienne took a deep breath. "I suppose the parish sheriff will look into his story again. They'll likely run into the same stumbling block—his alibi."

"Which was?"

"He'd taken Shayne's horse to an auction to sell. Plenty of people talked to him, and his signature was on the bill of sale." She frowned. "There was no way to make it add up. Trey had a nervous breakdown during the investigation, and Rick insisted we keep him in our employ until he left on his own. So I've had to look at that punk all these years."

Julienne's cell phone rang, and she excused herself with a whispered apology and a slight bow before turning away to answer. She held up her end of the conversation with terse answers and hung up without saying goodbye. When she turned back to me, tears brimmed in her eyes.

"Some evidence was found with my daughter's remains. Sheriff Braezeale will bring it by and see if anyone can identify it." Without waiting for me to answer, she led me out of her chambers.

SILENCE REIGNED in the library as we waited for the sheriff to join us.

Ricky spilled out of a delicate antique chair, his thick legs straining against the wooden armrests. He checked his cell phone often, occasionally tapping out a text message.

Madeleine sat on the brocade couch with her mother, their hands clasped together. The poor girl's eyes darted around the room, never settling on one spot for long. She caught me watching her and gave me a shaky smile.

I sat in a velvet-upholstered chair with a high back, and Dean sat on the chair's matching footstool, leaning against my legs. I massaged his tense shoulders, which did absolutely no good. I understood. The tension in this room was almost tangible. Though I longed for a smoke, I didn't dare shatter the brittle silence by excusing myself. Besides, I liked to think Dean needed me.

After the most strained half hour I've ever passed with strangers, the doorbell chimed. Ricky leapt to his feet and hoofed it to the door. After a hushed conversation, he returned with Sheriff Braezeale and a uniform I recognized from the crime scene. Both men nodded to Dean, and Julienne stood to greet them. She shook their hands, thanking them for coming out so late on the family's behalf. She offered them refreshments. *Did this woman ever lose her genteel grace?*

After refusing Julienne's offers, the sheriff cleared his throat and said, "This item was found with the remains. It is evidence and must stay in this plastic evidence bag." He glanced at each person in turn until he or she acknowledged the instructions. "Just tell me if you've seen this before or know where it might have come from. Or why the victim had it in her possession." Again, he waited to see if we understood his instructions.

Once he was satisfied, his gaze rested on me. Dread thudded in my chest. "Miss Mace? While I understand there's no way you could have known the victim, we need confirmation you know nothing about this item. It's just a formality, mostly for our paperwork. Miss Madeleine, you'll be doing the same thing." The two of us nodded.

The younger deputy approached Ricky and showed him a small item in a plastic bag. Ricky leaned forward, squinting at the bag's contents. "I've never seen that before." He slumped back in the chair and held his forehead in his hand, shaking his head. He began tapping out a message on his cell phone.

Seeing what he was doing, the sheriff placed a strong hand over Ricky's arm. "Please don't tell anyone what you saw in the bag."

Ricky nodded and stuffed his phone into his pocket.

Madeline confirmed she knew nothing about the item in the bag. Julienne took longer, leaning over the item and asking the deputy to hold it under the light. Though he obeyed her requests, she shook her head, her eyes shining with tears.

"I just don't know. I've never seen that before." She stood, her hands clenched into fists. "May I be excused?"

The sheriff agreed, and Julienne fled the room. Her sobs were audible from the hallway.

It was my turn. Leaning forward with curiosity, I wanted to see what this thing was. The younger deputy came near and held the bag in my sightline. In it lay a bronze coin about the size of a half dollar. The coin bore the words "Good for 1."

One what? I met the deputy's eyes and shook my head. Dean who had been jittering next to me the entire time, stood for his turn. He leaned over the bag and flinched.

"Do you have a flashlight?" His eyes moved between the two law officers.

The younger man took out a large metal flashlight and handed it to Dean, who clicked it on and peered at the coin. "Can you turn this over? Is there anything on the back?"

The deputy looked to his superior who nodded. He flipped over the bag and held it in front of Dean who again used the flashlight to peer at the coin. Finally, he clicked it off and sat back on the footstool. He rubbed his face with both hands.

"Turgeau?" The sheriff crossed the room. "You seen this before?"

"I have," Dean said. Ricky gasped and leaned forward in his chair. Madeleine mumbled something under her breath. My heart pounded so loud, I couldn't hear what she said.

"Well?" The sheriff put his hand on Dean's shoulder and squeezed.

"Trey Sorenson once owned a coin very like that." Dean's voice shook. "I thought he was investigated and cleared twenty years ago—"

"The case is no longer inactive. We can't tell you the details, and we'll ask you to keep any details you know to yourself." The sheriff's dark eyes crinkled around the edges, and he gave Dean's shoulder another squeeze. "Does Mr. Sorenson still live in his room in the barn?"

"Yep." Ricky stood. "I'm going out there with you."

"No." The old lawman's voice held enough force to make me jump. "You'll sit back down and let us do our jobs. Please don't make me invoke the rights of my office, Richard Junior."

Ricky sat back down, his face scarlet and a vein pounding in his thick neck. He exhaled a shaky breath. Dean approached him, leaned down and whispered in his ear. Ricky nodded, and Dean went to the bar, mixed him a drink, and took it to him. The law officers left without another word.

9

"Will they arrest him?" Madeleine's eyes widened, and her gaze moved between her older brothers. "I can't believe this. Trey's been part of our family since I was a baby."

"He's not part of our family," Ricky roared, slopping amber-colored liquid from his glass.

"Ricky, calm down." Dean's quiet words took the bluster out of his brother. Shoulders rounded, Ricky drained his drink and crossed the room to make another. His shoulders hitched a few times. When he returned to his seat, his eyes were red and shiny.

"Maddy, you know Shayne dated Trey during the last year of her life." Dean sat down next to his sister. "We can't know why his belongings were with her body."

"So he's a killer?" Madeleine clutched Dean's hand.

"Who knows?" Ricky drained his second drink in one gulp and rested his eyes on me. I saw resentment lurking there. The wound of Shayne's disappearance had healed and scarred over, and now it seemed my meddling opened it again.

"What was the coin?" Wanting Ricky's scowl off me prompted the question as much as inquisitiveness. His temper set off alarm bells in my head. I knew men like Ricky, men who ran hot and cold, one minute laughing, the next ready to fight.

Dean spoke up. "Trey owns a coin collection he inherited from his father. There were several coins like that. Trey claimed they were credit tokens from whorehouses."

"So they were valuable?" I didn't believe for a hot minute Trey would bury part of a coin collection. *Maybe he didn't do the burying.* In which case, someone framed him. Someone who hated him. Who hated Trey? *Uhhh, Ricky?* I pushed down the thought. Ricky no more murdered his sister than Santa Claus did.

"Trey thought the whole collection was valuable, but I have no idea." Dean shrugged. "He talked about selling it and using the money to start his own horse training business. But his father left the coins to him, and they at least had sentimental value."

"I remember those stupid coins now." Ricky snapped his fingers. "So that was one of them?"

The doorbell sounded again, cutting off any answer he might have gotten. Ricky jumped up and raced out of the room to answer it. He returned with the two officers.

"Trey's not back there, folks," said the sheriff. "Any ideas where he might be?"

Dean shook his head. "He's a heavy drinker, so probably out drinking, but I'm not sure where he hangs out."

"We'll check the area bars. Anywhere else?"

Nobody spoke.

"If he does show up, call us. Don't try to detain him yourselves." The sheriff's eyes rested on Ricky, who flushed. With a nod, the lawmen left.

"Mom and Dad should have fired him years ago." Ricky waited for one of us to agree. When nobody said anything, he stood and exited the room without another word. Madeleine, wide-eyed at the drama, excused herself, leaving Dean and me alone in the room. He fiddled around at the bar, finally pouring himself a bourbon and sitting next to me on the uncomfortable sofa.

I thought back to my conversation with Julienne. She called Trey a punk and was ready to say something else when her cell phone rang. Had her word choice simply formed out of her frustration? Or was there something else? I asked Dean.

"Really?" He wrinkled his nose. "I don't have a clue why she'd call him a punk. Ask her."

That went nowhere. I kicked off Madeleine's uncomfortable shoes and flexed my numb toes, trying to work feeling back into them. The display with the *Disappearing Culture* books caught my eye, and I decided to try again.

"Earlier, when Colton told me about the *Disappearing Culture* project, Shayne's ghost knocked the book out of my hand. She did it when he mentioned interviews."

Dean raised his eyebrows and set his whiskey aside.

I contemplated the raised eyebrows. Were they a warning to shut up now or risk an ass chewing? Only one way to find out. "Do you remember her having problems with any of the people she met during the project?"

"Not at all," he said. "She loved working on it, talked about it all the time."

"Did Colton go with her on the interviews?"

"Maybe some, but not all." Dean pulled off his tie and stuffed it in his pants pocket. "Shayne knew people in the community, and Colton was an outsider. Sometimes they'd talk more openly if Shayne went alone."

"What did Colton do on the project?" I remembered his name in the place of honor on each volume of *Cajuns: The Disappearing Culture.*

"Everything. Colton and the kids working on the project took over an unused classroom. I remember going to pick Shayne up on a Saturday." He smiled, but I noticed tears brimming. "They had papers and pictures piled everywhere. Colton showed me how he was deciding which pictures went with what interview. It looked like a huge amount of work."

"How did Colton get involved with your family? You said he was new to the community back then." I curled up against him on the sofa. Despite the spring day's warmth, night brought a damp chill to the old house. Dean rested his arm across my shoulders.

"Ricky and Colton met in college. They were in the same fraternity." Dean traced one finger down my neck and leaned in to nuzzle it. I elbowed him away.

"The only thing that makes any sense is Trey killing your sister over a lover's quarrel. And, from what your mother said, the timeline didn't work."

"Maybe something got overlooked back then," he said. "What did Mom want anyway?"

"Your grandmother's necklace. I was wearing it."

Dean pulled back from me.

Ouch.

"She asked me to use my ability to solve your sister's murder."

Dean, who had asked me the very same favor, only nodded. My heart twisted. I hated the fact I made him so uncomfortable. In big picture terms, I wondered if it meant I was wasting my time in this relationship. Would he ever come to terms with me being different? After all, it wouldn't change any time soon.

The room's pristine relics somehow linked the past and present. Shadowy flickers hovered in my peripheral vision, and it felt like the warm mahogany walls closed in on us. The feeling of someone watching crunched my nerves into sharp edges. A cold ghostly hand closed around my arm, and I yanked away and leapt to my bare feet.

"I think I'll go to bed." My whole body trembled, and it took all my effort to keep my voice even. Dean glanced at me and winced.

"I'm sorry. This is hard on you too." He smiled, surprising me. "And I bet you're starved."

"Huh?"

"You barely touched your supper. Not that I blame you." He motioned me to follow him out of the parlor and led me upstairs. "Us kids always kept a stash of junk food. Let's see what Maddy has."

I sent Dean along to Madeleine's room and stopped off

at mine to shed her dress and change into my spare jeans and t-shirt. On my way out, I took a look at myself in the mirror. Lisette had been right. I didn't belong here in this place, with this man.

DEAN HAD MADELEINE PEGGED. She kept a mind-blowing assortment of junky bakery treats in a plastic storage bin in her closet. Dean shoved them down one after the other, not even looking to see what he grabbed. Madeleine wolfed down an entire package of powdered donuts in a few seconds. I picked at a honeybun, fascinated as always by the way other people lived.

Madeleine sucked down half a bottled water and reached for a Moon Pie.

"You're going to have to put in double time in the club's weight room to work off all these calories." Dean unwrapped his own Moon Pie.

"I don't work out there anymore." Madeleine made a face. "Not since I heard the rumor about the peephole in the women's locker room."

"What rumor?" Dean ate half his Moon Pie in one bite.

"Back before my time, some tennis coach got caught using it." Her eyes moved between Dean and me. "The club fired him and repaired the hole. But they kept it hushed up so people would keep their memberships."

Dean choked on his food. Had I been eating, I'd have choked too. The serial killer Dean suspected of killing Shayne could have seen her scar through that peephole.

Dean, now red-faced, guzzled water out of his sister's bottle and gasped for air. I decided to question Madeleine myself.

"If they repaired it, why do you feel uncomfortable?" Dean and I exchanged a glance, and he nodded in approval.

"Oh, it's stupid." She shrugged.

"Tell us anyway," Dean said.

"A boy at school whose father works maintenance at the club said it wasn't repaired right, and he still catches boys peeping."

"Stay away from that place," Dean said. The eye contact we shared was worth a thousand conversations. All the years he spent believing Marcus Lewis killed his sister had been wasted time. If he'd known about the peephole, he could have looked at other suspects sooner. He ducked his head and glared at the floor.

"I hate to go off-topic, but what was Lisette going on about at dinner? And why did Mom act so funny?" Madeleine directed the question at me.

Dean raised his head to see how I'd respond. I raised my eyebrows, and he gave me a quick nod. I briefly explained I could see ghosts and how they sometimes wanted me to do things for them.

"Oh." She covered her mouth and blotches of red appeared high on her cheekbones. "I'm sorry I called my great-grandmother a witch in front of you."

"Why do you tell people that?" Dean scowled and then spoke to me. "She was just a weird old lady who knew about stuff before it happened. Not a witch. She died when I was a little boy."

A weird expression moved across Dean's face. I bet there was more to the story, but in front of his sister was not the time or place to try to draw it out. Until now, I thought Dean's aversion to my ability had to do with the psychic who shot him after he connected her to a string of murders. That shadow across his face added a new dimension to the story. Perhaps it went deeper than that.

"So tell me what ghosts want you to do. Solve murders?" Madeleine leaned forward, grinning. "That is so cool. I knew the second you got here you'd be cool."

Dean snorted, and I kicked him.

"So Shayne wants her murder solved?" Madeleine's words rushed out, no space in between for my answers. "Does she talk to you? Or can you read her mind?"

"Yes. No, and no." I tossed aside the honeybun and went to one of the impossibly tall windows. I opened it, lit a cigarette, and inhaled deeply, shivering as the damp air penetrated my clothes. Madeleine joined me and helped herself to a cigarette. I winced but said nothing. *Hey, those things aren't free.*

"Does Mom know you smoke?" Dean opened a Coke from Madeleine's mini fridge. He would never fall asleep after the amount of sugar he'd consumed.

"Mind your own business." Madeleine scowled at him and turned back to me. "Who do you think did it?"

"Trey seems a likely suspect, but if he has an alibi—"

"Don't tell my baby sister all that. It'll give her nightmares." Dean joined us at the window and made a show of fanning our smoke into the still night.

"I'm not a kid." Madeleine blew smoke in his face. "I mean, Trey wouldn't hurt us, would he?"

Dean grunted. "If he's responsible, he's probably long gone."

"Unless he didn't do it," I said. "In that case, he just went off to get drunk and feel sorry for himself."

"So he's a wild card." Madeleine dropped her cigarette butt into her empty water bottle. I did the same and closed the window. The three of us congregated at Madeleine's bed. I remained standing, ready to excuse myself and leave brother and sister to their visit. They didn't mind including me, but I felt like I just didn't belong.

Madeleine's next words stopped me. "I bet Lisette did it."

"The murder?" Dean sat down on the bed. "She did not. She and Shayne were best friends."

"I wonder how deeply she was investigated," Madeleine said. I snickered.

Dean frowned at us. "Lisette's not capable of that. I lived with her for fifteen years. She had her moments, but she's not capable of murder."

"Come on, Dean-o," Madeleine said.

"Don't call me that." Dean threw a stuffed pink monkey at her. She caught it and kept talking as though nothing happened.

"She was out for Peri Jean's blood tonight." Madeline tossed the monkey on her bed. "You can't tell me you didn't see that."

"Have to be blind not to," Dean said. "Lisette never left the high school mean girls mentality behind. It doesn't make her a murderer."

I didn't know what to say to that. Lisette outing me at supper disturbed me, but the way she acted when we were alone disturbed me more. That attack was more than "mean girls." My own disastrous first marriage left me with a lot of questions about the person I married. But it was a lot shorter than Dean's marriage. Was he unable to admit he married a monster? Dean slid off the bed and made a big show of yawning.

"I'm done," he said around another yawn. "Want me to walk you to your room?"

"Y'all better not let Mom catch y'all in there. This might be the twenty-first century, but she won't like it." Madeleine held the door open for us and closed it behind us.

MY HAND FOUND Dean's as he led me down the darkened hall and turned on the light in Shayne's bedroom before I entered. He followed me inside and pulled me to him. He brushed his lips over mine, and my knees turned to jello.

Dean broke the kiss and said, "I'm glad you're with me. Coming here hurts. I see all the things I couldn't do."

At first, with my head still swimming from his kiss, I didn't know what he meant. Then it hit me. *Shayne.* I tipped my chin to look into his eyes. "You were a teenager yourself when she disappeared. What could you have done?"

He shrugged. "But I became a fucking cop and still couldn't find out what happened to her." His hands slid from my arms. "My family expects perfection. I always figured they were disappointed."

"Listen to me." I grabbed a handful of his shirt and pulled him closer to my face. "You did everything you could. If they *are* disappointed, which I've seen no evidence—"

"You haven't met my father."

"Well, he's the one with the problem. Not you." I chose my next words carefully. I didn't want to make this about me, but I wanted him to know I understood. "My mom can't stand me for what I am. I spent a lot of my life trying to turn that around before I finally accepted it was out of my hands." I wrapped my arms around his waist and pulled him tight.

"Your mother is a fool." He smiled. "Having met her, I can say this with authority." He brushed his lips against mine. "You're the best thing I've got. Thank you for coming here."

I stood on my tiptoes and pressed my lips to his, my body tingling at his sharp intake of breath. Talking like this in an unfamiliar place made me feel very close to him. Closer than the—admittedly fantastic—sex we had. No man, not even the one I married, ever talked to me like this. Wanting to hold onto this feeling forever, I deepened our kiss.

Dean slid his hand under my shirt, his touch feather-light on my stomach, and backed me up to the bed. I let him push me backward and get on top of me. He traced my jaw with his fingertip, sending shivers through me. Desire and goose bumps tightened my skin. "When we first met, you spooked me." He leaned in to kiss me, cupping my cheek in one hand. "I'm glad I took a chance," he whispered against my face, his eyelashes tickling my skin.

"I thought you were a jackass." I wrapped my legs around him. "I'm glad I took a chance too."

We kissed, tongues entwined, hands roaming each other's bodies. I slid my hand under his shirt, caressing the hard ridges of muscle, thrilling at the warmth of his skin under my fingers. For that moment, it didn't matter who didn't want either of us because we belonged to each other.

OUR KISSES AND CARESSES INTENSIFIED, our bodies arching under each other's touch. Eyes locked on mine, Dean pushed my t-shirt up and popped my bra open. He took my nipple in his mouth, moving his tongue back and forth over the sensitive tip. I moaned and wove my hands in his hair, trying not to dig in my fingernails as need tightened between my legs. In the back of my mind, I wondered if this was an appropriate venue for a tryst. The thought faded away as Dean kissed me again and murmured against my lips, "I want you."

I wanted him too much to think about decorum. I reached between us and undid the button on his pants. Bracing himself on his knees, Dean tugged my jeans and panties down to my ankles, pushed down his own pants, and settled himself between my legs. At his movement, I became aware of a lust killer. The old bed squeaked. Loudly. Oblivious, Dean lowered his mouth to mine, pushed his hand between us, and teased me open with his fingers.

"Dean, I can't," I said against his lips. At first, he pretended not to hear, moving his fingers in ways that made my breath catch. After a few more seconds, I repeated myself.

He drew back from me, confusion clear on his face. "What is it?"

"The bed squeaks."

Dean, still breathing heavily, glanced around the room. "So? It's old."

"Your sister...she might hear." *Was that it? Or was there more?* Dean's angry words about my refusal to spend the night with him popped into my head. Maybe, deep down, I didn't want to have sex here because I couldn't go home to Memaw's house. Maybe after all the things we'd said to each other, I was scared of what the sex meant. By our own admission, this was more than an extended session of bumping uglies. This was real for both of us.

Dean watched me, his body bathed in the soft light the bedside lamp put out. "I'll stop right now, if that's what you want." Desire burned in his eyes, but hurt flickered there too, waiting for my rejection. My fears and insecurities made convincing arguments. If I put a stop to things now, my relationship with Dean would stay right where it was when I got here. If I didn't stop, things would get more complicated.

I stared at Dean and realized I wanted tonight to be different.

"I don't want to stop, but I want to get off the bed." Lust thrummed in me, but something more drove me. All the things we said to each other meant Dean felt the same way I did. I wanted this relationship with him more than I wanted anything else. I got off the bed, shimmied the rest of the way out of my clothes, and motioned him to sit on the window seat. Dean groaned as he realized what I had in mind and obeyed. His fingers burned against my skin as I straddled him and looked into his eyes. I traced his jaw line and ran my thumb over his full lower lip and lowered my head to kiss him, both of us inhaling deeply, trying to get as much of each other as we could.

He broke the kiss and whispered, "Now. Hurry."

I slid down on him and gasped. We moved together, drowning in each other's eyes. *I don't want to live without this man.* My pleasure built into a throbbing ache, and I put my hands on his cheeks to keep his eyes locked on mine. The intensity of it drove me over the edge, and I shuddered first, squeezing my eyes shut. Feeling this way was worth the risk of heartbreak.

Dean put his hand on the back of my neck and pulled me in for a kiss, sucking my tongue into his mouth, nibbling on it. I bucked against him, holding back a scream that would have woken the house, and he let out a strangled cry. Spent, we both relaxed, gasping together, the stubble on his chin digging into my shoulder.

"Spend the night in here with me," I whispered between gasps. "I want to be with you."

Dean drew back to look at my face, his eyes still half-lidded and sleepy with the afterglow of good sex. "You sure? That bed's little. You might sleep better alone."

My heart swelled at his kindness. This was my out if I wanted it. But I'd realized something while we made love. Distancing myself in this way wouldn't immunize me to heartbreak if our relationship ended. It was too late for that. Our connection terrified me, but I needed it. I needed him.

"Please?" I kissed the corner of his mouth. I got off him and held out my hand. He smiled and took it, letting me lead him to the bed and crawling between the sheets with me.

Dean's breathing deepened into the slow pattern of sleep almost immediately. I lay there, wide-eyed and full of what ifs, my body begging me for sleep after such an eventful day. Dean's arms tightened around me. He was mine for the night. Neither of us knew what tomorrow would bring, or even if we'd make it until the end of the week. *Perhaps the secret to life is about enjoying the good moments for what they are...moments in time.* I let my eyes close and drifted into the worst nightmare I've ever had.

10

———————

I LAY SOMEWHERE cold and damp, pain slamming in my head. The only light I saw in the inky darkness was a square of light somewhere above me. Disoriented, I tried to push myself to a sitting position, but something was wrong. Nothing worked the way it should have. My brain sent signals to my limbs, but they failed to respond. *A nightmare. That's all this is.* I tried to wake up and could not. I felt a bolt of pure panic.

As I lay shivering, a figure appeared over me. I tried to speak, to ask for help, but nothing came out other than a mumble. A hot, hard hand grasped my wrist and pulled something off my finger. Then the figure climbed down where I was and began covering me with scoops of something. It peppered over my skin and the fresh, damp scent hit me. Dirt.

A scream built in my chest but stuck there. I needed to let my dream tormentor know I didn't want to be buried because I was alive. But I felt paralyzed. More moans and mumbles escaped my mouth. The person burying me ignored them. The dirt covered my face, spilling into my mouth. I couldn't even turn my head to the side to spit it out. Eventually, the dirt covered me all over. Every time I tried to draw a breath, I choked on granules of dirt.

Above, I heard banging and hammering. I prayed for rescue. But then footsteps receded, and I heard a car start. My heart slowed, and I wondered if I could die in a dream and survive in the waking world. That thought scared me enough to wake me up.

I sucked in a loud breath and attempted to sit up. Icy hands pressing on my chest held me down. Whining and gasping, I struggled, but my attacker had the strength of the dead. I swung one arm out, fumbling for the bedside lamp. I clicked it on, and the room flooded with light. Crouched on my chest, her face inches from mine, was Shayne.

"Get away from me." My terror-stricken voice cracked and crumbled. I pushed at her, but my hands went right through her. I did the only thing I could think of to do. I opened my mouth and screamed so hard it scraped my throat raw.

Dean jerked awake next to me and turned to see what was wrong. He took one look at me struggling underneath nothing, and his mouth fell open, the color draining from his face. "What is it? What's wrong?" He reached out to touch me but drew back his hand.

"Shayne. She won't let me up." At my words, she faded into nothing. I sat up, shaking and gasping, as a flowery scent flooded the room. *I bet Shayne wore a perfume like that.*

"Where is she?" Dean leapt from the bed, sniffing like a hound. "And where did that smell come from?" He knelt and peered under the bed like a kid afraid of the boogeyman.

Despite the closeness we'd just shared, the old self-doubt seeped into me, poisonous and painful. *Is this part of my life too much for Dean? Maybe it's too much for anybody normal.* I drew my knees up to my chest, very conscious of my nakedness between the sheets.

"She's gone." My raw throat barely allowed me to speak above a whisper.

Madeleine knocked on the door, and we both jumped. "Y'all okay in there?"

Dean jerked on his pants and went to the door to talk to his sister. It took some convincing, but Madeleine went back to her room believing I'd had a vivid nightmare. Dean settled back in next to me but didn't fall asleep so fast this time.

"Can you smell that?" He pitched his voice low.

"Yes." I explained no further. He pulled me tighter against him and kissed the back of my neck.

"Was it her in your dream? Was it Shayne?"

"I dreamed her death. The killer buried her alive back there. The dirt was going into her nose and mouth, and—"

"It's all right. She's gone now." Dean stroked my arm, but his hand shook.

"I couldn't breathe. I was afraid I was going to die in the dream." *Should I tell him to go back to his room if he's too freaked out?* Maybe, but I didn't want to be alone. Not after that. "I was afraid I'd die in the dream and die here too."

Dean drew in a sharp breath, his body tensing next to mine. He took my hand and threaded his fingers through mine. "I won't let that happen. I'll wake you up if you're struggling."

The rest of the night passed with both of us falling asleep and jerking awake. When dawn poured through the windows, Dean kissed me. "Try to get some sleep, babe." He brushed my hair away from my face. "I have to get started working." I nodded and curled into a ball, the tenderness in his eyes a warm comfort.

After he quietly slipped through the door, the odor of Shayne's perfume hanging in the air made me think sleep impossible. I got up and sat in the brocade armchair near the window and tried to think of ways to lessen Shayne's power over me. Fear from the night before lingered in my nerves like a hangover, making me feel both nauseated and exhausted.

I jolted awake to full daylight streaming into Shayne's room and someone pounding on the door. I straightened in the chair and wiped sweat from my face. I checked my cell phone and saw it was nine-thirty. *How did I sleep after last night?*

"Yes?" I hollered at the door.

The door cracked open and Madeleine stuck in her

head. "Breakfast is in ten minutes. It's the best meal we have, the only one Mom doesn't cook."

Malaise evaporating, I bit back a smile remembering the scene last night with the cakes and donuts and Dean's and Madeleine's open dislike of their mother's cooking. It made the Turgeau family seem more down-to-earth. Or maybe I was getting used to the idea of this family, of having a rich boyfriend.

"I'll be there, but it may be more than ten minutes."

"Okay. I'll save you a muffin if it looks like things are going fast."

I pushed myself out of the chair, chuckling. Growing up in my grandmother's home as an only child insulated me from many experiences. Life as part of an extended family surprised me by being enjoyable. It almost made me forget the drama with Shayne's ghost. But not quite.

My clothes from the night before still lay crumpled on the floor. I shook them out and pulled them on. I stepped out in the hallway and realized I didn't remember how to get back to the main part of the house. I had been so busy playing fish out of water, worrying about what Dean expected of me and what I could deliver that I hadn't paid attention. I went back in my room—Shayne's room—and looked out the window, trying to decide which direction to go.

Back out in the hallway, no more sure of myself but a lot more determined, I headed in what I thought was the right direction. Before long, I found myself lost in a maze of hallways, leading to rooms obviously unused by the family. I made a disgusted sound. *This place is like the frig-*

gin' Bermuda Triangle. Amelia Earhart is probably in one of these rooms. In my peripheral vision, I caught a glimpse of swishing dark hair passing one of the open hallways. Awash with relief, I called out. No response. I charged in the direction of the only other living person in this part of the house and came upon her in an alcove nestled in one of the turrets.

"Hey, Madeleine. I'm so glad I saw you. I've been lost for twenty minutes."

The young woman turned. Registering the black holes where Shayne's eyes had been, I gasped and backed away, hands out, warding her off. The ghost had led me on a wild goose chase. No telling what she wanted with me in these hidden corridors. I spun and raced back the way I came. Three left turns later and I was lost again, more so than before. I turned down a hallway only to find Shayne waiting for me.

This time she raised those black holes to meet my eyes. I felt the sensation of falling, my stomach doing acrobatics, and couldn't pull my eyes away. Harsh whispers filled my ears, and I clapped my hands over them. I fled and took a right turn at the end of the hallway. Hearing voices, I sped up my pace.

"These last few days have made me wonder what I was thinking." I recognized the voice as Lisette's. "I want to try again."

My fear took the short leap to fury. I stalked toward her voice, moving fast even though I felt pretty sure I didn't want to see this.

"IT'S TOO LATE NOW," Dean said. "You need to figure out a way to be happy with your life. And leave me alone to work out mine." My heart sang at Dean's rebuff. I stopped in my tracks and held my breath, silently cheering him on.

"It is most certainly not too late." Lisette's voice raised. "I've known you all my life. I've loved you all my life. We just got a little messed up."

"If you know me as well as you claim to, you should know I don't move backward. I always go forward. Making the same mistake twice—"

His speech abruptly cut off with a lip smack. I charged forward, ready for battle. For someone so comfortable calling others trash, Lisette sure acted the part. I got there in time to see Dean shove Lisette away from him. She backpedaled and bumped into a wall. Her features tightened with malice. If humans could shoot laser beams from their eyes, Dean would have been toast.

"You son of a bitch." She shoved off the wall and launched herself at him, all teeth and claws. His head rocked back from a particularly hard slap, and he grabbed her arms and tried to hold back her blows, but did so gently. Fuck that. This bitch didn't need gentle. I waded into the fray.

I gripped Lisette's arm and yanked her away from Dean. "He's too much of a gentleman to fight you, but I'm not. You want to play slappy-slappy, try it with me."

"Peri Jean, don't. She's not worth it." He grabbed for me. I stepped out of his reach. My temper danced frantically, spurring me on, begging for action. I'd been waiting for this moment since last night in the dining room.

"Come on, Lisette. You afraid to fight someone who'll hit back?" I put my hands on my hips. "I'll let you go first."

"You don't scare me." She bared straight, cosmetically whitened teeth at me. "You're just a trailer trash whore Dean feels sorry for."

"Pot, meet kettle." I had to laugh at her.

"What is that supposed to mean?"

"Your marriage to this man ended because you cheated on him. I may have done a lot of shit, but I never cheated on anybody." I glanced at Dean, who jerked as though slapped. *Uh-oh. Going too far, Peri Jean.*

"You told her our business?" Lisette hissed at Dean. She curled her hand into a fist and advanced on him.

"Lisette, I'm warning you." I doubled up my own fist, which had a lot more battle scars than hers. "Hit him, and I'm going to hit you back."

The sound of Lisette's open palm on Dean's face dominated the small space. I launched myself at her, my arm coming up on instinct and catching her across the throat. I drove her into the wall hard enough her teeth clicked together.

"Don't touch me, you nasty little thing." She managed to get an arm free and clawed my face. The new cuts burned.

That was it. I wound up and busted her in the nose. Her eyes widened in shock as she put her hands over her nose. She moaned in pain. Blood oozed through her fingers and dripped down her pristine outfit. I backed away from her since she didn't seem inclined to continue our little monkey dance. I bumped into Dean, who pulled me farther back.

"Are you okay?" He examined the claw marks on my face and grimaced. "That's going to be nasty."

Lisette emitted a bubbly gasp. "I think she broke my nose."

"It's not broken." Dean didn't sound sympathetic at all.

"Put some ice on it." The tone of my voice probably pissed her off more, but I couldn't help myself. She acted one way in front of Julienne and another way to people she considered beneath her. Had things ever not gone her way? Or was this the first time anybody stood up to her?

"You're not going to tell me what to do, you...I don't even know what to call you." Her stuffy nose voice tripped my giggle box. She flushed an even deeper red, tears shining in her eyes. She turned from me and spoke to Dean. "Really. She's attractive enough, but can't you find a little classier woman to see to your needs? I mean, someone who sees ghosts? Dean, what are you thinking? You hate that sort of thing."

I took a step toward her, and she flinched. Her body trembled, but I didn't think it was fear. This was rage. She slipped one hand into the pocket of her elegant slacks and withdrew an expensive smart phone.

"I'm calling the sheriff, pressing charges."

That made me even angrier.

"It doesn't matter if you press charges or anything else. If I kick your ass, it'll happen before your shitty cavalry arrives." I stomped toward her. Hands closed around my middle and yanked me away from Lisette.

"Stop it, Peri Jean." Dean's breaths came in gasps as I struggled against him. "Just cut it out. Get out of here. Go somewhere and cool off." He gripped my arm and whispered in my ear. "I'll keep her from having you arrested."

The green-eyed monster in my mind wondered how he'd do that. I didn't want him pandering to his awful ex-wife. Was that worth staying out of jail?

"Come on," Dean said. Deep in his blue eyes, glee sparkled, and I grinned. He wouldn't pander to her. I didn't know what he would use to make her see things his way, but I'd let him handle it.

I shot Lisette the stink eye and stomped out of the room...and right into the dining room. Madeleine and Julienne sat with their mouths open, obviously having heard the commotion. The new scratches on my face throbbed. I wondered if they looked as bad as they felt.

"Sorry," I mumbled and fled the room.

11

———

DESPITE THE DARK clouds hinting there'd be more rain, the front lawn was alive with workers hauling away more debris from the storm. They all turned to look at me when I stepped out onto the wide front porch. Though they had no way of knowing the drama that just occurred inside, their stares felt accusing. I jogged down the steps and cut around the side of the house, headed toward the area where I found Shayne's remains. Had it only been yesterday? It seemed like an eternity.

My cell phone rang. The caller ID showed a goofy picture I took of Dean. I rolled my eyes and answered.

"Wait for me," he said.

I turned to see him on the porch holding a paper towel wrapped around something or other. My stomach growled, and I desperately hoped it was food of some sort. I jogged back to him and held out my hand. He pretended offense but handed it over anyway. I wolfed down the first sausage and biscuit without tasting it and nibbled on the second while we walked.

"That went quick. She calling the sheriff?"

"Hell, no. She assaulted both you and me before anybody laid a hand on her." Dean inhaled his own biscuit and licked his fingers. "For another thing, her little show last night at the dinner table pissed me off. I know how she finds out stuff like that. It's not illegal, but the way she uses the information could get her in trouble."

"How *did* she find out that stuff about me?" I'd wondered, but then got more interested in getting laid and forgot to ask Dean.

"She keeps a private investigator on retainer. One call to Gaslight City would have done the trick." Dean frowned. "You told me yourself the townsfolk love their gossip."

I reeled at the idea of Lisette paying a private investigator to check up on me just so she could use what she learned for hatefulness. From the sound of it, she had a rich husband, a luxurious life. Why waste time on me? "Why is she like this?"

"Low self-esteem. Her mother was, and still is, an abusive drunk. Lisette's father left and her mother turned the full force of her abuse on her."

"I almost feel sorry for her."

"Don't," Dean said. "I made excuses for her the entire time we were together. I thought there was something redeemable underneath the bitch act. There isn't."

A few seconds later, Lisette marched out to her car, her hand over her face. She saw us watching her and shot us the finger. We returned the favor. Formalities complete, she got into her car and sped away. A bolt of lightning lit the sky, punctuating her exit.

I thought back on my relationship with my childhood best friend Chase. I tolerated him long after most people would have cut him off for being unstable and a pain in the ass. Perhaps living with him for fifteen years would have turned me off for life. *You'll never know, Peri Jean, because you got him killed.* Desperate to get away from the thought, I asked Dean the first thing that popped into my head.

"Is your mother going to be upset I bloodied Lisette's nose? She loves her like a daughter." I liked Julienne and hated the idea of her disliking me.

"And she knows her like a daughter. Lisette's temper is legendary at our house."

"So I beat the shit out of her, and nothing's going to happen?" I had a hard time believing that. Julienne controlled her house with an iron fist, and I figured she wouldn't take kindly to me causing a brouhaha here.

"Not exactly." Dean stuffed the paper towel in his pocket and avoided my eyes. "I told Lisette to say she lunged at you, tripped, and busted her nose."

I didn't picture Lisette just going along with it.

"What'd you do? Threaten to tell your mother y'all's marriage ended because of her stepping out on you?"

"Empty threat. She knows I'd never do that." Dean watched his feet as we walked along. "I spent fifteen years splitting up and getting back together with that woman. I know enough about her to fill one of those tell-all novels. The private detective shit is just scratching the surface."

We walked along in silence. I couldn't understand why Dean wouldn't tell his family about his ex-wife's screwing around. He obviously didn't like her being here. That would be the perfect way to get rid of her. Was this a male pride thing? I gave Dean a sidelong glance. Perhaps it was.

He prided himself on doing everything well. He performed his duties as a sheriff's deputy back in Texas with kindness and bravery. When he ran for fitness, he ran fast and looked good doing it. He was an excellent lover. My body tingled at the thought.

The way I figured it, Lisette's cheating on him implied he wasn't a good husband, maybe not a good lover. It embarrassed him. He didn't want anybody to know he'd failed. At least not that way.

Seeing one of Dean's vulnerabilities made me feel protective of him. I'd really kick Lisette's ass if she gave me the opportunity. If I felt this strongly about Dean, why did admitting it to myself scare me so much?

The core issue slammed into me, almost knocking me backward. *It's the face he makes when anything to do with me seeing ghosts comes up.* Over the past six months, he'd looked at me that way several times—a mixture of terror and revulsion. Last night, I saw it again.

My mother rejected me because I saw the spirit world. Would Dean eventually do the same? He might love me, but he didn't love everything about me. Did that make our relationship a sham, something that could never work, no matter how we wiggled and danced? I swallowed hard as I remembered last night.

I didn't want to live without him in my life. That was the bottom line.

Dean stopped walking, and I took a few extra steps before I realized it and came back to him. He had his head cocked to one side, frowning. I heard the high-pitched whinnying of the horses in the barn.

"I swear I let those horses out to pasture this morning," he said. "If they're back in there, it means Trey's back. Just stay here." He walked off.

I ignored his words and followed him into the huge structure. He didn't even bother to glare at me. He knew by now I wasn't the obedient type.

Judging by the distress in the horses' whinnies, I expected a ruckus inside the barn, horses bucking, their eyes rolling and teeth bared, the whole nine. Instead, the barn fell quiet the second we stepped inside. Dean drew a handgun out of his belt and put his finger to his lips for me to be quiet. Sometimes his carrying a weapon at all times disturbed me. This time, I felt grateful.

The smell of shit dominated the close, stale air. A gust of wind picked up outside, and the big building groaned, raising chill bumps on my arms. Thunder boomed outside, rattling everything inside. One of the horses snorted and fidgeted within his stall. I reached in to scratch his long face. Something was off in here. I could feel it.

Dean crept down the long line of stalls, his footsteps crunching in the hay covering the floor. I tensed, waiting for Trey to reveal himself. Perhaps the Namadie Parish Sheriff's Office found him and took him in for questioning. In the depths of the barn, something clinked together. My nerves twisted into a painful ball. The sound reminded me of stereotypical ghosts rattling chains.

Adrenaline flooded my veins, spurring my heart into double time. My fingertips tingled, begging me to take some sort of action. A horse snorted, and I almost screamed. Now Dean was at the back of the barn, nearly invisible in the shadows.

Wind hit the barn again, and a rhythmic creak accompanied the metallic sound. I glanced up at the high ceiling, expecting to see a pulley for hay. I saw nothing like that.

Dean stopped at the last stall, his mouth hanging open, his handgun pointed at the floor. After a second, he re-holstered the gun but continued to stare. I couldn't stand it and went to see what he saw. It couldn't be dangerous. Otherwise, he wouldn't have put away his pistol.

I couldn't see what had Dean so upset until I stood next to him. Trey hung at the back of the empty stall, a rope knotted around his neck. He had looped the rope over an exposed beam, and his feet hung less than an inch from the floor, his toes nearly touching it. I gasped and stumbled backward, covering my mouth in horror. The overpowering odor back here made my hastily eaten breakfast rebel. I gagged, and Dean snapped out of his stupor.

"Not in here." He grabbed my arm and pulled me toward a door marked exit.

"It's okay." I tugged my arm out of his hand. "I won't ralph in here."

Another gust of wind blasted through an open window in the stall and set the dead man swinging again. I realized the metallic clink was the cuff of his denim jacket brushing the brass button on his jeans. The creak was the rope moving. Unable to help myself, I took a good look at Trey. His eyes bugged out of his face, and his skin had turned black. I thought I'd never forget those two details.

A white slip of paper was pinned to his jacket. Curiosity outweighing my horror, I leaned forward, trying to make out the words. I read aloud, "I can't stand it anymore. I am sorry."

A suicide note? What couldn't Trey stand? And what was he sorry for? I backed away from the corpse, wondering where his ghost was, if it was doing whatever ghosts did to make themselves appear to me. My chest tightened at the thought. I didn't need to see another ghost, especially not with Dean standing next to me.

The horses shuffled in their stalls and made high-pitched sounds. I peered into every dark corner, expecting to see Trey's ghost. Animals might not be able to speak, but they weren't dumb. They sensed something wrong.

I peeked into an open doorway at the end of the hall and found what looked to be a combination office and bedroom. Trey must have lived here. Papers were scattered over the desk. I tiptoed forward.

"Don't go in there," Dean said.

"I'm not touching anything. This is my only chance to satisfy my nosiness. Besides, after that show you put on yesterday, St. Namadie Parish Sheriff's Office won't be sharing info with you."

Dean grunted and followed me into the office. Together, we looked at the mess.

"These are the letters Shayne wrote him," Dean said. "He showed them to me years ago, when I was still married."

"So...he started reading them and got depressed?"

"I don't know. The note said he was sorry. Maybe, after her body was dug up, he knew it was only a matter of time before his connection to that coin came out."

"But what about his alibi?"

Dean shook his head and shrugged. "We need to get the sheriff out here. He needs to see this." He grabbed my hand.

We turned to leave the sad little office, and I bleated. Standing in the doorway were Trey—a much younger and more handsome Trey—and Shayne. Next to me, Dean let out a yelp of shock. *So he sees them too. How the hell? Crud, crap, and shit.* Questions about why and how crowded my thoughts, but I pushed them away to focus on the worst part of it all. This was the thing Dean hated about me. I couldn't even look at him. I just yanked him toward the ghosts and led him through them.

My bravado earned me a blast of their indignation to my solar plexus. It spread through me and knotted my muscles. I lowered my head and bulldozed forward. Once we reached the fresh air outside the barn, my muscles loosened.

Dean and I faced each other. His breath came in gasps. His tanned skin had gone ashen, and a sheen of sweat stood out on his face. He jerked his arm out of my hand and put his hands on his knees and stared at the ground. I crossed my arms over my chest and braced myself for his reaction.

"You see that all the time?" He raised his head to stare at me. His hands trembled as he took them off his knees. Self-doubt stuck its sharp claws into me and drew blood.

"I'm sorry you saw them." *Sorry? Dammit, dammit, just dammit.* I couldn't help being this way. If I could, I'd get rid of my connection to the spirit world. I tried to think of logical reasons this might have happened. *Is Dean's seeing the ghosts a side of effect of what happened to me six months ago? Maybe his connection to Shayne made me a conduit.*

Dean stared at me, his face still so pale I thought he might pass out. "I just can't believe you live with it."

"It's worse since that night six months ago." I shifted foot to foot. Dean and I never discussed my cousin's murder or the way it got solved. He carried his own demons from the experience. Me, I knew talking it to death wouldn't change a damn thing.

"I hope I never see one of them again." Dean said the words to himself more than to me. I jerked as though slapped. It was possible the longer he hung around me, the more likely he'd see something else horrible. I hung my head and tried to pull it together. Dean put his hand on my back, and I shrugged away from his touch.

"I'll go up to the house and tell Mom and Maddy not to come down here. You call 911." Dean hurried past me.

When he got out of sight, I took a few shuddering breaths. *Don't you dare cry, Peri Jean.* It wouldn't solve anything. Besides, I couldn't spend the rest of my life being such a damn baby over this. It was my cross to bear. Shoving my resolve into place, I reached into my pocket for my cell phone and touched warm metal. *No. Not again.* I knew what I'd see even before I pulled my hand out of the pocket. Sure enough, Fayette's necklace dangled from my fingertips. Remembering the black opal folklore Julienne mentioned, I let out a disgusted groan. *This necklace again. What the hell is this thing? Could it cause Dean to see his sister's ghost?* I couldn't even begin to imagine, I realized, and shoved the necklace back in my pocket.

Wishing I was home, I closed my eyes and clicked my heels together three times. Nothing happened.

12

———

TREY'S DEATH caused a bigger upheaval than the discovery of Shayne's remains. Julienne melted down. She and Dean and Madeleine holed up in the library making phone calls. This time, I didn't bother giving her back the necklace. Why make things worse?

I wandered Dean's family home, the weird necklace swinging on my chest, tingling where it touched skin. I bet if I stopped in front of one of the black-spotted mirrors and pulled it out of my t-shirt, veins of electric color would be flashing through it.

The weird little thing found me everywhere I went, somehow moving itself place to place. It was magic, a magic I didn't understand, didn't know how to learn. The necklace and its magic represented the thing Dean didn't like about me, the reason my mother rejected me.

The necklace should have scared me, dammit. But it didn't. It felt right hanging around my neck. Every once in a while, I caressed it, reveling in the warmth of the little shocks bolting through my fingers.

In a musty corner of the old house, I found a hallway lined with paintings covered by old sheets. I peeked at a few and immediately saw why they hung in an unused part of the house. Not every artist of yesteryear was all that great. Or maybe the people were uglier.

I knelt to look at an accent table, and the hallway grew icy. Vapor steamed out of my mouth, and dread scratched at my raw nerves. I stood too quickly and overbalanced. As I tried to right myself without messing something up, Shayne appeared next to me.

"What do you want?" I said. "You won't show me how to help you. I can't solve your murder if you don't do that. Why don't you just move on?"

She disappeared. *Thank goodness.* It was too easy, but I wouldn't look a gift horse in the mouth. I continued on my path, once opening a door to peek inside at the plastic-protected furniture. I walked inside the room, drawn by an antique cheval which, for some reason, was uncovered. Those always caught my attention.

I stared at myself in the dust-hazed old glass, pulling the magic necklace outside my t-shirt and watching the colors move in it. The sight mesmerized me. When I refocused, the person on the opposite side of the mirror was no longer me. It was the necklace's original owner, Julienne's grandmother, Fayette. She looked exactly as she did in the painting in Julienne's suite. I stumbled backward, and the woman's ghost stepped out of the mirror and winked at me.

Fear set my heart galloping. Its hard thumps blurred my vision, jarring Fayette's ghost. My knees buckled, and my back bumped a dresser, dislodging a dusty silver dresser set, which crashed to the floor. Fayette's lips curved into a smile. I heard her laugh in my head. Cold sweat broke out over my body.

"You want to see? We'll show you." The voice was all around me and nowhere at the same time. I moaned, unable to speak, my chest aching with fear. It was the first time I'd heard a ghost speak other than a word here and there in whispers. As though called, the whispers started. Fayette and I were no longer alone.

WHILE I STOOD FROZEN in terror, the room filled with every kind of ghost imaginable. Some wore clothes I associated with movies like *Gone with the Wind*. Others wore even older styles of clothing, things I'd seen in history books about the Revolutionary War. A few of the ghosts were African American and wore ragged clothes I associated with slaves. Shayne and Fayette planned this attack, brought friends. I made a silent promise to never verbally antagonize a ghost again.

I fought my way to the door, struggling to escape the icy hands grabbing and pulling at me. Pathetic mewling sounds came from my throat as I fought against the ghosts. Nobody could hear me scream in this forgotten corner of the house. What if the ghosts decided to keep me now I could hear them? Finally, they released me.

I hurried down the hallway, my heart leaping into my throat with every beat. Rounding a sharp corner, I came face-to-face with all of them. Dead arms reached for me. Mouths opened to display blackened teeth and emit moans I knew would make up the soundtrack to later nightmares. I backed up, only to be pushed away from a ghost I'd bumped into. I turned to face the one who'd pushed me, and it was Shayne. The familiar face did nothing to comfort me.

"In there." Dean's sister gestured at a closed door, her voice echoing inside my head. Wild horror clawed at my sanity. Hearing them speak scared me more than any other dealings I'd ever had with the spirits. Feeling a flash of impatience from Shayne, I turned my attention to the door.

It bore inches of dust and cobwebs. No way did I want to go in there. They might trap me in there. *Forget this shit.* I ran in another direction, only to find another cadre of ghosts waiting for me. I carefully backed away from them, lamenting my foolish curiosity about this house.

Shayne gestured at the door again. I didn't see any way out of doing her bidding. Tentatively, I reached out and tried to turn the doorknob. It was locked. Relief flooded through me. Now I wouldn't have to go into some unknown, dark, and dirty place. But my relief was short-lived.

Shayne motioned at our ghostly audience. Fayette, still wearing her pageboy haircut and flapper dress, pushed her way through the crowd. She dropped a skeleton key at my feet and winked at me again.

Seeing no other option, I picked up the key and used it. The door opened like magic, as though the lock had been recently oiled. The hinges didn't even squeal. A stairwell ascended to parts unknown of this huge, weird house. I glanced at the ghosts surrounding me, and they pressed forward, again reaching their cold, blue-fingered hands toward me. I fled up the stairs, my footsteps dislodging thick dust on the stairs. The door shut by itself, cutting me off from not only my spectral fan club but the rest of the world.

NOBODY HAD BEEN up here in some time.

The stairs ended in a tiny room furnished with a dilapidated chair bleeding stuffing out of rips in its upholstery and a little round table. With a little spiffing up, the duo would have cost a fortune at Silver Dreams Antiques back in Gaslight City. I studied the room, trying to figure out my job up here.

On the table sat a half-full bottle of whiskey and an empty glass. Neither had been touched any time in the recent past. Dust obscured the bottle's label. An equally dust-covered book sat next to the chair. I brushed off a thick layer of dust from the book on the table. Tiny motes flew into the air, sparkling in the weak sunlight streaming through the attic window. My nose gave a warning tickle, and I braced for the sneeze. It hit with force, and I sneezed several times in rapid succession, bumping the table on which the book sat in the process. It tumbled to the floor, knocking the rest of the dust off and sending a card sized paper flying over the floor.

"Great," I hissed, kneeling to pick up my mess. With the dust knocked off, I saw the book wasn't really a book but a bound report of some sort. I glanced at the first few pages and realized it was Shayne's pet project, *Cajuns: The Disappearing Culture*. Because I hadn't had the chance to look through the book in the glass display case, I leafed through the pages, reading a paragraph here and there. Interesting stuff, but I couldn't believe Shayne had me chased into this room to see it.

The piece of paper that had flown across the room caught my eye, and I bent to pick it up. It was a picture showing a gorgeous, smiling Shayne next to Trey. On the the back, inscribed in decidedly male handwriting, was written "I will love you forever." *How sweet.* I thought I might go into sugar shock.

Still not wanting to sit in the nasty chair, I leaned against the wall, which was no less nasty. This little room had obviously been Shayne's secret hideout. She came up here and drank illicit whiskey and mooned over her boyfriend. And now both of them were dead. A shiver passed through me.

"I still have no idea what you expect me to find up here," I said aloud.

Shayne materialized in a corner of the room, her form flickering in and out of my vision. Other shadows roiled in the room's corners. I didn't look too closely at those. Shayne knelt next to an overturned crate and moved her hands around the bottom of it. Cringing, I joined her on the dirty floor.

I lifted the edge of the crate and found a dusty plastic makeup case, the kind I remember storing my own makeup in when I was in high school and college. Shayne vanished, taking the other shadowy figures with her. *Good.* At least I could concentrate.

I opened the box and gasped at the pile of junk inside it. Letters folded into origami shapes stuffed the top trays. The handwriting on the letters matched the writing on the back of the photo I'd found. Each letter was addressed to "Pookie" and signed "Punky." Disgustingly cute. *These must be companions to the letters Trey left on his desk.*

I set the letters aside and sifted through the rest of the box's contents, finding a stale bag of marijuana, a broken charm—the kind that fit on a charm bracelet, and a wad of scarves at the box's bottom. On top of them sat a slim volume full of loopy girlish handwriting. It had to be Shayne's journal, diary, or whatever kids called them twenty years ago. The makeup box was a treasure trove of information, but I wondered which piece was important.

Not the letters. If Shayne's appearance with Trey's ghost meant anything, it was that he didn't kill her. Someone, however, had buried Trey's coin with Shayne. Who would do that and why?

The charm meant nothing to me. The marijuana couldn't help me. The journal had to be my clue.

I sat down in a corner of the filthy room and started reading.

13

I CRACKED OPEN THE JOURNAL, hoping for a page that read "so-and-so killed me." Of course, it's never that easy. And it's always painful and odd finding out other people's secrets. There was usually a reason the secrets were secret.

The first page of the diary got right into the thick of things.

My name is Shayne Fayette Turgeau, and I bought this book to talk about the person I hate most in the whole world, Lisette Marie David. She is just awful.

Wow. So much for Shayne's friendship with Dean's ex-wife. If Shayne hated Lisette, why had she continued any kind of relationship with her? Family pressure? Social pressure? Only one way to find out.

I skimmed through a junior high entry about Lisette getting angry and passing a rumor that Shayne had head lice. It didn't surprise me. Despite Dean's talk about Lisette having a hard home life, no excuse existed for her kind of nasty.

I flipped through the book, just reading a few sentences here and there. The entries followed Shayne the remainder of junior high and into high school. Though more and more time passed between entries, the accounts became more and more disturbing.

Today was the worst. Lisette came home from Cancún bragging about losing her virginity to some stranger. She cheated on my brother and expects me to think it is great. I threatened to tell Dean what she did. She begged me not to tell, to let her come over here tonight and talk to me about it. Try to talk me out of it is more like it. This time, she's gone too far. Dean loves her, and this will hurt him. But what if he marries her? He told me they're applying to the same college in Florida. I can't stand the thought of her just treating him like shit. I want to tell him, but will he hate me for being the one who hurt him?

Shayne and Lisette's talk must have been more of an argument. The next entry, dated a few days later, documented the price of standing up to Lisette.

That bitch. She passed a rumor that I stayed home over spring break because I had an abortion. Everybody now knows Trey and I slept together. Now that we've broken up, I feel so stupid for having done it. Things are miserable here at school. Someone wrote baby killer on my locker. For all I know, it could have been Lisette herself. And I didn't even tell Dean about her cheating. I can't hurt him like that, not when he's so in love with her. But the other thing is I'm scared of her. I've seen what she can do when people cross her.

Another entry revealed the extent of Lisette's willingness to make Shayne miserable.

Someone—one guess who—put garbage in my locker. My

books are ruined, and I had to go around all day with sour milk splashed on my new jeans. Mom is going to be furious. Do I tell her about what's going on with Lisette? Mom loves her like family. Lisette's family, even though her mother is a lush, is part of our social circle. I wish I could ask Dean for help, but then I'd have to tell him why she's angry at me, and it would break his heart. But maybe telling him she cheated on him would be best. She's doing all this to try to scare me out of telling him. If I told him because of it, it sure would be ironic.

The final entry chilled me the most.

Today was the last straw. Lisette said she wanted to make up and brought me iced sugar cookies from Slice of Heaven Bakery. I believed her because I want our feud to be over and ate them all. After lunch, I got so sick I threw up. Mrs. Simmons saw me get sick in the girl's room and took me to the nurse's office. When I started talking about patterns and flashing lights, the nurse called Mom. She freaked and took me to the hospital. They said I'd been doing drugs, probably LSD or mushrooms. Mom's mad as hell, doesn't believe I didn't take the drugs on purpose, and I'm grounded. Lisette must have dosed those sugar cookies. I'll keep her secret about cheating on Dean, but I won't be her friend any more. Never ever.

The entry was dated April 19, 1991. The newspaper article in the library said Shayne disappeared several days after that, on April twenty-fifth. The hair on the back of my neck rose. I set the journal aside gently, even though I wanted to throw something. What an awful existence for a teenage girl.

After witnessing Lisette's fuckery over the past day and a half, I was willing to believe her capable of anything. *But murder?* The horror of the idea notwithstanding, I doubted Lisette had the physical strength to kill someone of equal health and fighting skill.

Or did she? Shayne could have slipped and taken a fatal fall, or any number of things that would have left her dead and Lisette panicking. If Lisette was willing to slip her an LSD mickey, she might have drugged her and...I didn't want to imagine the rest. Shayne lured me into this room for a reason. She wanted me to find this journal of terror. It had to mean something.

I tried to imagine how Dean would react to me accusing Lisette of murdering his sister. *I need proof.* Dean liked to have all his facts and figures straight. The first time he took me on a real date, he had everything planned down to the moment he took my clothes off. I shook away the memory. *Not now. Too distracting.*

After more than twenty years, where would I find proof Lisette had anything to do with Shayne's disappearance? I set the book aside and fingered the scarf lying across the box's bottom. The fabric had a metallic gold thread woven through it. Very pretty. I wondered why Shayne left it up here. I pulled it from the box and drew in my breath at the layer of micro cassette tapes lining the box's bottom. I picked up one of them, the label on the jewel case reading "*Traiteur* interview. 2-25-91." The interview tapes from Shayne and Colton's project. I opened the tape case even though I had no way of listening to them and found a slip of paper folded into a tiny square tucked inside.

It was a receipt for the sale of a used computer to some random person. The receipt was initialed, but the handwriting was so horrible, I couldn't tell what it said. *Why would Shayne have that?* I packed both the receipt and the tape back into the case and put the cassettes back into the box. The Turgeaus would probably love to have them as a remembrance. But for now, I'd leave them be.

My wild goose chase ended, I needed to figure out a way to connect what I'd learned about Lisette to Shayne's murder. *If I just had a piece of proof, something to shake her up.*

As I struggled to stand, the journal slipped from my fingers onto the floor. I picked it up and noticed something written in the back cover. I held the book open and squinted at the scratchy handwriting, obviously Shayne's but written while she was upset or in a hurry. A list of names stretched down the back cover. I recognized the names from the tapes I'd found in the bottom of the makeup box. *Traiteur* was circled. To help her remember where the receipt was? Try as I might, I couldn't see the purpose of the list.

I bumbled out of the of the attic room, ready to be away from this dark, lonely hideout. I locked the attic door behind me and slipped the key into my pocket. Then I set about finding my way to Shayne's old bedroom. When the teenager's ghost appeared and motioned to me, I followed more gratefully than I cared to admit.

I FOLLOWED SHAYNE, who knew the big house much better than I, down several unused hallways. She stopped in front of a bookcase and pointed to a lever beside it. I turned the lever, and the bookcase clicked open, revealing an unlit passageway.

The dim light from the hallway barely put a dent in the darkness. A damp, mildewy smell wafted out at me. *How many secrets does this place hold?* I would have never noticed the lever next to the bookcase had Shayne not pointed it out. Devoid of enthusiasm, I followed her down the corridor. I didn't trust her, but I also didn't want to be left alone in there.

Cobwebs tickled my face, and a couple of times I heard something scurrying on the floor. By the time we reached the end on the hallway, the hair on the back of my neck stood on end, and I wanted a shower. Light flooded into the passageway from a keyhole. It was enough for me to see the knob and pull the door open. I found myself in a coat room with another closed door facing the one through which I entered. *What the hell?* I'd wanted to go back to Shayne's bedroom to plan my next move.

Voices drifted in from the next room. I walked to the other door, knelt, and peered through the keyhole. Julienne, Dean, and Lisette sat in the parlor. All of them held drinks. Lisette's nose had swelled quite nicely and purple half-moons hung under her eyes. I smiled, but one look at Dean's surly expression killed my mirth.

"You said you wouldn't press charges on Peri Jean." Outrage stripped away the good old boy accent he usually employed.

I sucked in a shocked breath. *Press charges? Oh, that*

bitch. I bit back a string of ugly words begging to burst from my mouth.

"My husband was insistent." Lisette managed to turn down her lips and manufacture a sigh. All for Julienne's benefit, no doubt.

A cold hand closed around my arm, pulling me from the drama in the parlor. Shayne gestured at a big, red purse hanging on the wall. Had to be Lisette's. Too ugly for Julienne. Too big for Madeleine.

I pitched my voice low. "I am not touching her belongings."

Shayne's anger filled the room. The purse quivered against the wall for a few seconds and began to swing. When it gained enough momentum, it bounced off the rod and hit the floor, right side up. Shayne's apparition appeared next to the purse and kicked it. The purse flew over on its side, spewing its contents on the floor.

No, no. Lisette already wanted to press charges on me for popping her a good one. This would only make things worse. I fell to my knees and stuffed the junk back into the ugly red bag, trembling in my hurry to not get caught. Shayne slapped each thing I picked up out of my hands, but then gestured for me to pick up something else. I crossed my arms over my chest and shook my head. Shayne grabbed my ear and nearly yanked out my earring. I cried out before I could stop myself.

"What was that?" Julienne's voice drifted in from the parlor.

I crouched low on the floor, like doing so would make me invisible if someone opened the door.

"Some of that junk you've got sitting in the cloak room." Lisette laughed. Neither Julienne nor Dean joined her.

I rose to my knees, listening for the creak of someone getting out of a chair. Once Dean went back to trying to cajole Lisette out of pressing charges, I stood. And elbowed a coat rack. The stupid thing bounced against the wall and then hit every single fucking thing in the room before it rattled to the floor. Footsteps walked across the parlor. I felt the fingers of cold dread worm its way through me. I was so busted.

Shayne motioned to an old, tooled leather zippered purse, one that might store coins. I shook my head and whispered, "Too late."

Shayne's cold fingers danced over my ear again, fumbling for my earring. I ducked out of her reach and grabbed the pouch off the floor. When I did, a shiny piece of metal tumbled out and hit the floor where it bounced.

The door swung open and Lisette peeked into the room, her big mouth open to say something witty. Seeing me, her eyes widened and darkened with rage. "Where did you come from?"

The item from the coin purse finally tumbled to a rest, the metal pattering against the floor like a drumroll. I grunted in surprise when I recognized Shayne's ugly emerald and ruby ring, the one I'd seen in the painting, the one I felt someone take off her/my finger in that awful, vivid nightmare. *How ugly.* Heaven help me, it looked like a damn watermelon. I looked for Shayne and found her standing near the door from which we entered the room, a smile on her face.

"Who is it?" Dean walked across the floor and peered around her.

About that time, Lisette saw the ring and sprang into action, trying to get to it before I could. I scooped it up and stuffed it in my jeans pocket. Shoving Lisette out of way, I spoke to Dean. "I need to talk to your mother."

"Give me that." Lisette grabbed at my arm.

"I'll kick your ass all the way to New York City if you touch me again." I held my hand over my pocket, afraid she might try to reach in there and get the ring. I elbowed my way out of the closet, ran across the room to Julienne, and handed her the ring. Lisette thundered along behind me but stopped cold when she saw who had the ring now. Her face turned a particularly satisfying shade of gray.

"I might have some explaining to do, but I think you have more." I crossed my arms over my chest. "Why don't you explain how you ended up with a dead girl's ring?"

14

LISETTE TRIED to smile at Julienne, but she looked like she was about to hurl. Julienne examined the ring and set it on the table next to the love seat.

Still poised, she asked, "Why do you have my daughter's ring?"

"I bought it a pawn shop the summer after Shayne disappeared."

Julienne gasped. Dean's mouth opened and closed, his eyes wide. He said, "You *what?*"

"I bought it at a pawn shop in Houston." Lisette dragged each word out, enunciating each syllable. *Smartass.* I wanted to kick her in the hoo-ha.

"I understood you the first time. I just can't believe what I'm hearing." Dean rubbed his face and gave his head a quick shake. "How did you have Shayne's ring the entire fifteen years we lived together and not tell me about it?"

This must have been how they sounded when they fought. Part of me wanted to be somewhere else. I didn't want to see the side of Dean who once lived with this woman. But I loved train wrecks and couldn't look away.

"It's not Shayne's ring." Lisette raised her voice. "It's *my* ring. It had nothing to do with you." She widened her eyes and shrugged.

"Don't play innocent." He swatted the air in her direction. "We both know you're not."

Lisette snorted at Dean. She might as well have dared him out loud to expose her running around like a cat in heat. My mouth itched with longing to out her. I squirmed, doing everything but putting both hands over my mouth. Lisette turned on me.

"I can't believe you snuck in there and went through my things." She pressed her lips together, arranging her face into a sympathetic expression. "It might be difficult for someone like you, someone from a broken home full of murderers, to understand why that was wrong, but it was. I feel sorry for you."

I fumed, and one hand curled into a fist. I wanted to rear back and knock that self-righteous look right off her face. One glance at Julienne told me I couldn't do that. I had to play this right or risk looking like that bad guy. Or girl.

"You're one to talk about doing the right thing." I raised my eyebrows at her.

"Peri Jean, I assure you I have never, ever gone into someone's purse and taken stuff out of it." She pulled her shoulders back, trying to regain her composure.

"You've done worse. Let's talk about Shayne." I rushed the next words, trying to get them out before Lisette had a chance to speak. "Why don't you tell Shayne's mother and brother the stuff you did to her the last few weeks of her life? The rumors? The garbage in the locker? Any of that sound familiar?"

"You shut up." She bared her perfect teeth at me. A vein pulsed at her neck. Forget that cool as iced shit routine. I fought not to smile.

"I found a diary of Shayne's upstairs." I directed this to Dean and Julienne, making eye contact with each of them in turn. "In it, she talked about the way the original Mean Girl here terrorized her from junior high until the time she died. There's some damn interesting stories in there."

Shaking her head, Lisette turned away from me and spoke to Julienne. "She's lying. Don't listen to her."

Julienne all but waved her away, her attention focused on me.

"You remember getting upset with Shayne because you thought she'd done drugs at school?"

Julienne put her hand over her mouth and nodded.

"Lisette doctored her food. Brought her sugar cookies from some bakery. Sliced Heaven? No. That's not right."

"Slice of Heaven," Dean said. "Shayne loved their iced sugar cookies."

Julienne gasped and stared at Lisette with her mouth open.

"You want me to tell them what y'all were fighting about, Lisette?"

"I am warning you. Shut. Up." Lisette faced me now, leaning forward with her fists clenched at her sides, her body tensed like an animal about to launch itself at prey.

"You have no business in this room, in this house, with my ex-husband."

I smiled, and her face went white. "Do you think you'd still be welcome here if they knew what I know about you?"

Lisette leapt over the coffee table the way King Kong rose over the Empire State Building, hands outstretched and curled into claws. Adrenaline and a lifetime of fist-fights took over. I grabbed her hand and yanked her past me. Her momentum carried her into the wall. She slid to the floor and screamed a hoarse, pain-filled cry at the high ceiling. She turned to us, her face twisted into a hideous caricature of fury.

"Yes," she gritted out. "I knew it was Shayne's ring. And I didn't care why it was at the pawn shop." She slapped her hands down on the floor in front of her. "She had every-thing, everything I wanted. This family, this house. People who really loved her. I wanted someone to love me the way everybody loved Shayne."

Lisette wilted, her dark eyes filling with tears. Her lips trembled, and her face twisted as she began to wail.

Dean goggled at his ex-wife and glanced at his mother and then at me, as though for confirmation this was really happening. We stared at Lisette as her crying turned into half-hysterical shrieks. Julienne Turgeau covered her face. Her soft sobs played like background music.

Dean grabbed the ring off the table, stalked over to Lisette, and knelt in front of her. She took her hands off her face and stared at him with wet, wide eyes.

"I did love you. But you cheated on me with every one

of my friends. You cleaned out our bank accounts, and I lost the house because of you."

Julienne gasped. I was too riveted to the horror show in front of me to react.

"You knew it was wrong to have this." Dean shook the ring in his ex's face. "Otherwise, you wouldn't have hidden it from me our entire marriage. Why are you like this?"

Lisette rose. Walking a little unsteadily, she went into the coat room. She knelt in full sight of us all and pushed her belongings back into her purse, her shoulders shaking with silent sobs. She got control of herself and wiped her face with a white, lacy hanky. Finished, she stood and walked into the parlor, stiff and self-righteous.

"I'm glad this is finally over." She spoke to Julienne. "I wanted to tell you so many times why Dean and I broke up."

"It's far from over," Dean said. "You broke the law when you bought this ring and didn't turn it over to the police. They might have been able to go back to the pawn shop, track down the killer. But, because you can't think about anybody but yourself, you obstructed justice. I'm calling Sheriff Braezeale. You'll tell him what you remember."

"The hell I will," she said. "Let me leave right now, or I will rake your family's name through the mud, destroy your reputation."

"You're not going anywhere." Dean stood in front of the door, his arms crossed over his chest. He motioned me to stand in front of the other set of double doors leading out of the parlor.

Lisette marched toward me, and I doubled up my fist. "Think I won't hit you?"

She gasped and narrowed her eyes. "You are so low class."

I reared back my fist, but Julienne materialized next to Lisette and gripped her arm hard enough to illicit a whimper. "Go sit down. Now. We are going to call the sheriff, and you're going to tell him everything you remember about obtaining my daughter's ring. And when you are finished, you will leave my home—and this ring—and never come back. Do you understand?"

"I can ruin your reputation in this community," Lisette had the nerve to sneer.

"Call your lackeys on me if that's what you need to do. But who do you think people in our social circle are going to believe?" Julienne leaned into Lisette's face. "Me, a well-respected member of this community, or you, the neurotic daughter of a drunken whore?"

Lisette said nothing more and went back to her chair. Dean called the authorities.

JULIENNE, Dean, and I stood at the parlor window and watched Lisette waving her hands at Sheriff Braezeale, who looked twenty years older than when I first met him. No doubt she was trying to convince him she didn't need a ride to his office to make her statement. Finally, shaking his head, he gestured toward her Mercedes and got into his cruiser and eased down the driveway. Lisette sat behind the wheel of her car and reapplied her makeup as though the sheriff wasn't waiting for her to follow him to his office where he may or may not arrest her for obstruction of justice. I wanted to laugh at her, but it wasn't funny. Not really.

"Was she ever investigated for the murder?" I spoke to Dean, but Julienne answered.

"She was at cheerleading practice. The other kids, the faculty sponsor, all saw her."

"And I saw Shayne during those hours," Dean said. "She was upset, twisting her ring, and I teased her about it. She went for a walk. I never saw her again." His voice broke on the last sentence.

"After cheerleading practice, Lisette helped me cook supper," Julienne said. "By the time it was ready to eat, we figured out Shayne was missing. She didn't have a chance to do it."

Silence took over the room. Dean hunched his shoulders and frowned. Julienne played with Shayne's ring.

"I wish Shayne had lived," Julienne whispered. "I wonder what she would have done with her life."

"Probably the same as all of us," I said. "Did some things she wished she could take back. Did some things she was proud of. Wondered what to do in between. But she'd have been alive."

"I miss her every day," Dean said.

Julienne and I both looked at him standing there with his hands shoved in his pockets. I stroked one arm, and he pulled me into a hug.

"I am sorry," I said into his ear. Breaking the hug, I

spoke to Julienne too. "I owe both of you an apology. I caused major upheaval in your family and didn't even solve Shayne's murder."

"Don't say that." Julienne sat on the love seat. Dean and I followed and took a seat on the hard-as-a-rock-but-beautiful antique sofa. "We can put some sort of closure to Shayne's disappearance. Maybe we'll catch the killer. Maybe we won't. But this is a form of closure. All those years, I worried she'd been kidnapped."

"Me too." Dean turned to me. "Especially after I went into law enforcement. The things human beings do to each other." He took my hand. "Sometimes I'd wonder what happened to Shayne. Almost drove me crazy. Besides, I think you'd have found your way down here one way or the other."

Puzzled, I stared at him.

"The day I left Gaslight City, I forgot my wallet because..." He trailed off and shook his head. "Never mind."

"No," Julienne said. "I think something made Peri Jean join us this week, and you're going to tell us what happened."

Dean hunched forward, digging his elbows into his knees and wincing, probably at the pain it caused his injured leg. "After I signed off patrol, I went home and got out of my uniform." He glanced at me. "You know my routine. I take off the pants and then empty the pockets onto my dresser. Well, that day, before I could do that, I heard someone scream my name. A woman. She said, 'Help me, Dean, please help me.' I swear that's what I heard. I yanked my pants back on and ran outside. Nobody was there." Chillbumps rose on his bare arms.

"When I came back in, an old photo album I hadn't even unpacked was laying on my bed. It was full of pictures of me and Shayne as teenagers. Ended up, I got distracted and then had to hurry. Anyway, I broke my routine and forgot my wallet." He snorted and shook his head. "I hate stuff like this, stuff I can't explain."

So he did. But I thought he loved me. Our eyes locked and a little understanding passed between us. His eyes told me what he loved about me was enough. I felt tingles of elation. For just a moment, I was willing to believe in unicorns and pots of gold at the end of rainbows.

Julienne slipped Shayne's ring onto her finger and held it up.

"Here's my story," she said. "The night before Rick hurt himself, I had a dream, and I rarely dream. In the dream, Shayne brought a friend home from school, a little black-haired girl." She glanced at me. "She introduced her as Terry. But now I think she may have said 'Peri Jean.' So I think she wanted you here, to help us settle things and move on. Perhaps Lisette will finally help solve Shayne's murder. Though she couldn't have done it, no telling what she knows."

I couldn't help remembering Shayne's reaction to Lisette's humiliation. It hadn't been one of relief. Shayne took spiteful pleasure in the whole scene. After reading her journal, I understood why. But I also wondered if that little drama hadn't been an "Eff you" from beyond the grave.

"I really hope Shayne can rest now," Dean said. "And, if she isn't satisfied, she needs to act quick."

"Why is that?" Julienne said.

"Because me and Peri Jean are going back to Gaslight City. Tomorrow morning. I called Ricky while Lisette and Sheriff Braezeale were screaming at each other. He's coming over. We'll do as much as we can. But Alicia wants him home for the weekend. The boys have sporting events to get to."

"That's the right thing to do, son." Julienne nodded. "Your daddy can damn well live with not having things exactly as he wants them. This place'll get cleaned up— and things put back to rights—when it gets done."

I had forgotten about Dean's father in all the hoopla. "How is he doing with...everything that's happened?"

"Raising hell. Furious not to be part of it." Julienne snorted. "You just wait until you meet Big Rick. He makes Dean look lighthearted."

"That's the truth." Dean stared at the wall, lost in some memory. When he turned back to me, he had a smile on his face. "Go pack your things. Let's go home."

We exchanged a smile, that secret smile only lovers share. Even though he didn't love everything about me and never would, I wanted to be with him. Things would play out between us the way they did. That's all life was, really. Just a chance for things to go the right way.

"There's one more thing." I spoke to Julienne who turned to me and forced a smile on her exhausted face. I took off the necklace and handed it to her with a weak smile. "Sorry."

She laughed and shook her head. "Don't be." She took the necklace and slipped it into her slacks pocket.

I skipped out of the room, for once not lost. It sucked because just as I figured this place out, it was time to go home.

15

———

I MADE my way back to Shayne's room. The nagging sensation I'd missed something wouldn't leave me. I tried to ignore it because I wanted to go home. I couldn't wait to see Memaw and tell her the less freakout-worthy parts of this little vacation. I'd been away from her too long, missing out on the precious little time we had left.

I set my overnight bag on the bed, leaning it against the wrought-iron headboard, and took one more good, long look around the room. There was nothing here to tell me what happened to Shayne. Maybe nobody would ever know.

I gathered my belongings off the dresser, rolled up the dirty t-shirt I'd worn the day before, and tossed it all in the bag. As I untangled the cord on my cell phone charger, the overnight bag leapt off the bed, did a somersault, and hit the floor, scattering junk everywhere. *Not this again.*

"Shit!" A breath of cold air tickled the back of my neck, and the feeling of someone behind me crawled over my skin. This time I felt more disgusted than frightened. Time for me to tell her I was done. "Shayne? Listen to me. Your brother is important to me, and I care for him. That means I care about you too, but we've gotta get back to our lives in Gaslight City. I don't know what else I can do."

The bedroom door slammed, shaking the pictures on the wall. The force made my overturned duffel bag jump on the floor. Shayne's fury, white hot, mingled with my irritation. I couldn't let her goad me into anger. Taking deep breaths, I slowly let go of the emotion she poured into me. I spoke to the empty room.

"If you can't show me what I need to solve your murder, let us go. Let your brother be happy."

Shayne's fury hit me, knocking me back a few steps. The force of it frightened me. Could she hurt me right now? Kill me? *Probably.* I don't think she wanted Dean to be unhappy. But she died young and would forever possess the understanding of a sixteen-year-old girl.

"Come on, Shayne. Show me." I softened my voice, hoping to reason with her.

The bookshelf scooted away from the wall and tipped forward. My heart jumped into my throat. *Mistake. Never encourage a ghost to act out. How would I ever adjust to the new intensity in my connection with the other side?* I breathed a sigh of relief when all the books stayed in place except for one. A slim volume slid to the floor and landed fanned open.

I cautiously approached, expecting it to fly at my face. A yearbook dated 1991, the year Shayne disappeared. I turned over the book and found it open to a full-page picture.

The picture, though only a snapshot, had been blown up to fit the whole page. The caption underneath the picture read "This year's Panther Yearbook is dedicated to Shayne Turgeau, who disappeared April 25, 1991, the day this picture was taken."

The picture showed Shayne sitting at a table in the school library, big, old-fashioned headphones on her head, her micro cassette recorder beside her, and a typewriter in front of her. The ring Lisette bought from a pawn shop flashed on her finger, the matching necklace at her throat. I wondered what had happened to the necklace, if it had ended up in a pawn shop, too, but then noticed the stack of micro cassettes next to Shayne. *Bingo.*

Shayne wanted me to listen to the cassettes. *Took me long enough to figure out. No wonder she's pissed off.* I rolled my eyes and caught a flash of Shayne standing in the bedroom's doorway. With both hands fisted at her hips and one foot cocked out to the side, she looked like a frustrated teenager. A deep sadness took my breath away. She died so young.

She didn't live long enough to get to the point where she wondered about the part she played in her own misery. She died at a time when she still thought she could take on the world. This last revelation put me no closer to solving her murder, but it forced me to think about my own choices.

I took a deep breath. "Fine. Let's go listen to those tapes."

LONELINESS and the smell of dust clung to Shayne's hide-out. I stood for a silent moment in the dark little alcove, mourning the girl who never got to come back up here, who never got the chances I'd had to make things right. This time, I didn't snoop around. I just grabbed the plastic makeup case containing the cassettes and beat it out of there. The thought of staying made me feel incredibly sad.

I found Nadine dusting a monstrous antique mirror in the entry hall. As I approached, she acknowledged me in the mirror and said, "No matter how hard I try, this thing always has dust sticking to it. Must be all the in-and-out traffic. The missus won't hear of doing away with it. Been in the family since the War Between the States."

"This place is amazing." I wanted to cut to the chase, just ask Nadine if the Turgeaus owned anything as outdated as a micro cassette player, but this was the first time she'd spoken to me like a human being. "Parts of it are like a time capsule, but the modern stuff mixed in makes it feel alive."

She tucked her feather duster into the waistband of her maid outfit and looked me over. "Mr. Dean and Mr. Ricky are oversee'n the last of the work outside. Want me to take you to 'em?"

"No, thank you. Would you happen to know if the Turgeaus keep a micro cassette player? One of those little bitty ones? I know they're outdated, but..."

"Honey, look around this joint. This bunch don't throw nothing away." Nadine threw back her head and laughed. I joined her. When she finished, she said, "Come on. There's one in the library, and you're already familiar with that room."

A few minutes later, Nadine set me up on a soft leather chair with a scratched micro cassette player and a package of batteries.

"Just listen till your heart's content." She strode to the door but turned back to give me another long look. To my surprise, she said, "I'm sorry I laughed at you when we first met. It was un-Christian of me. Mr. Dean's a serious one, but I can tell you make him happy." Without waiting for my answer, she exited the room, leaving the door half open. *Well. How about that.*

I really didn't have time to ponder Nadine's change in attitude. Heart pounding, I fumbled through getting the cassette player working and played the first tape. It was nothing more than an interview conducted by Shayne with a person whose speech pattern suggested they had few or no teeth. Between that and the thick accent, I had a hard time following the conversation.

As the minutes ticked by, I played two more tapes and grew more frustrated. Whatever Shayne wanted me to understand evaded me. Noticing the cassette labeled *Traiteur*, I picked it up and re-examined the receipt inside. In the better light, I could tell the middle initial of the scrawl was either a J or an I. *Big help.* The first and last letters still looked like ripples on a pond. Then I remembered how Shayne had listed the title of each tape on the back of her journal. *Traiteur* was circled.

I pushed the tape into the cassette player and clicked it

on, expecting an immediate answer. But this interview was just like the others. It contained nothing out of the ordinary. I set the player on a leather ottoman and paced the room, only halfway listening to the serious young woman who sounded so much like a female Dean asking interview questions and approached the display of Shayne's pet project.

"Last accomplishment she ever made," I muttered as I leaned over the display. Opening the glass cabinet's sliding doors, I grabbed the first book in the series and flipped to the table of contents. Most of the interviews I'd listened to were listed. I set that book down and picked up the second volume. Its table of contents listed interviews I hadn't seen in Shayne's tapes. It must have been published after her death. The only book she actually worked on then, was the first volume. I picked it up and looked at the opening pages.

One thing jumped out at me. The first page read that Colton James Starr conducted all the interviews and processed them. Shayne Turgeau was listed as his assistant. I flipped to the interview section and noted again Colton was listed as the interviewer. Not Shayne.

Odd. From what I could tell, Shayne conducted these interviews alone. Of course, Colton could have supplied the interview questions and sat in on the interview. But it didn't seem that way. Shayne built on the conversation and asked questions about specific points no set of interview questions could have anticipated. I put the book back in the glass case and walked over to sit on the leather chair again, still barely listening to the interview.

The conversation between Shayne and her interviewee ended, and the woman said she had a gift for Shayne. Iced sugar cookies. In her excitement, Shayne must have forgotten to turn off the recording function. The tape hissed through Shayne saying polite thank yous and walking to her car. The car started. The deep groan of a door opening filled the small space.

"Shit." Shayne dropped the polite teenager voice and sounded like a real kid for the first time since I started listening. "You scared me."

"Been waiting on you to get finished." There was a pause punctuated with the smacks of kisses. "Let's get out of here before they come out to see what you're doing."

I matched the male voice with what I remembered of Trey's voice. The car's engine changed pitch as Shayne shifted gears and began driving.

"You been in my room in the barn lately?"

Shane let out a coquettish giggle. "You mean since the last time we were in there?"

"Yeah." Trey didn't share Shayne's flirty tone.

"The last time I was in there was Friday night." Shayne sounded hesitant, nervous even. I didn't know her well enough to know if she was lying. "And, as you'll remember, we were together."

"Oh, I remember that, all right. You sure you telling the truth?"

"Why don't you just tell me what this about and let me respond to that?" I didn't have to know Shayne to identify the fear in her voice. I felt scared for her. This didn't sound good.

"Pull off up here, in that driveway. Nobody lives there anymore."

Don't do it, girl, I thought.

The car's engine settled into an even hum as Shayne shifted into Park.

"What's this about, Trey? You're acting like I did something wrong, and I didn't."

"Somebody stole my daddy's coin collection." Trey's voice carried a reedy, accusing edge. Though I hadn't known him at all, it tightened my skin into chill bumps. When Shayne spoke, her voice shook.

"You have to know it wasn't me. I know how important your father's things are to you. I've never touched them other than the times you've shown them to me."

"Think your brothers did it? What about that pretty boy teacher always sniffing around you?"

Colton. He had to mean Colton. I leaned forward as if to coax the words from the piece of technology.

"I can't imagine my brothers doing it."

"That leaves your boyfriend, that damn teacher. He's just a user. I can see it in him." Trey's voice dropped to a menacing growl. "He know about them coins?"

"Mr. Starr is not a user. He just loves history." Shayne's voice wavered.

It certainly wasn't a no. In fact, it was almost a yes. My mind fluttered around, trying to fit the information I had together.

"Interested in history, my ass." Trey huffed a nasty snort. "Those coins are missing, and I know you can tell me where they ended up."

"I can't." Shayne sucked in a shaking breath and let out a half sob. "Mr. Starr would never steal your coins."

"You're gonna get those coins back." Trey's weight shifted. The vinyl on the car seat squealed. Shayne cried out, and I flinched. He had hurt her somehow.

"Let go of me!" Hysteria filled her demand. My fists clenched as I listened to the struggle and Shayne's sobs. I heard a thump and the groan of a car door opening. Shayne screamed, "Get the fuck away from me. Don't ever come near me again, or I'll tell my brothers what you just did. I'll tell them you fucked me too. They'll beat the shit out of you and get my parents to fire you."

I hoped she'd kicked him in the family jewels. He deserved it. Richly.

Trey, his voice strangled as though he was in pain, said, "You stay the hell away from my room in the barn, you spoiled little tramp. If I ever catch you down there again, I'll—"

The tape came to its natural end and cut off.

I sat in the leather chair, hands shaking, cheeks burning with hot anger. Something, an answer, hovered at the edge of my mind. Fury that Trey had accused Shayne, the way he had terrorized and brutalized her, kept me from reasoning it out. The library door swung the rest of the way open. I jerked to my feet in surprise and struggled to compose myself as Colton strolled into the room.

He took one look at my face and said, "Am I interrupting something?"

"No. I found these tapes that Shayne made while the two of you worked on the *Disappearing Culture* books. On this one, she forgot to turn it off after the interview, and I heard her and Trey have an argument." I didn't mention the questions I had about Colton taking credit for the interviews. The Turgeaus thought a lot of him, and it would only brew hurt feelings.

"Oh?" Colton, hands in his pockets, strolled over to the display and stared at the contents.

"Yeah. He accused her of stealing some coins his father gave him. Got physical when she wouldn't admit to it."

Colton, his back to me, made no response. Realization finally slammed into place. The brothel coin found with Shayne's body, the one the entire Turgeau family claimed belonged to Trey, had been stolen. Unless he lied when he accused Shayne. I thought back to the rage in his voice and dismissed the idea. If Trey's coins were stolen before Shayne's murder, then someone else left them with her body. The real killer. Trey thought Colton took them.

My throat tightened as other pieces fell into place. The credits inside the books claimed Colton James Starr conducted the interviews, but he didn't. He stole them from Shayne. I remembered the telephone conversation Julienne overheard.

Then I remembered the receipt in the cassette case. The initials on the bill of sale for the computers took shape in my mind. That middle initial was a J, not an I. And the first and last initials were C and S. Colton James Starr. Shayne kept that for some reason. Had she spent the last days of her life building a case against Colton?

Colton turned to face me and frowned at the expression on my face.

"You look so serious. You figured it out, didn't you?"

I sucked in a breath and tensed to run.

"Don't try to leave." He took a switchblade from his jeans pocket and hit the silver button. A wicked length of sharpened steel flashed out. He walked from the display to stand in front of the one door leading out of the library.

"Nadine!" My scream echoed back at me. "Nadine!"

"She's outside beating the rugs. Now you'll want to come with me."

"Fuck you," I spat, breathing hard. "Go on and kill me here. Then you'll have the mess to clean up before anybody finds you."

Colton moved toward me. *Oh shit*. Was he going to try to kill me? Adrenaline surged. I scrambled for a stalling tactic.

"Why'd you bury the coin with Shayne?"

"That's a pretty good question. Trey's coin collection wasn't the windfall I hoped it would be." He sneered. "That particular coin was rare but only worth thirty or forty bucks. Figured it would go a long way toward framing the little turd if Shayne's body was ever discovered."

"Did Shayne figure out you stole the coins? Is that why you killed her?"

"She—"

I ran for the door. In a tackle that would have made a football player envious, he slammed me into one of the built-in bookcases. The edges of the shelves dug into my ribs. The air whooshed out of my lungs. Colton used his belt to secure my arms at my sides while I gasped for oxygen. I screamed, and he punched me in the head.

Dazed, I barely struggled as he pulled a crusty hanky from his pocket and stuffed it in my mouth. I gagged but fought for control once I realized throwing up in my mouth would kill me.

Unable to fight, struggling to breathe, I went along for the ride as he dragged me right out the front door. The area, teeming with workers just that morning, was deserted. The work had moved to the back of the property. I heard Nadine beating rugs back there. She was so close, yet she could have been a million miles away. Colton stuffed me in his trunk and closed it on my muffled pleas.

16

───────

THE STUFFY DARKNESS of the trunk and my thundering heart made it even harder to catch my breath. Colton started the car engine and drove away from the house, gravel rolling and cracking beneath the wheels. The sound smoothed when he turned onto the blacktop road in front of the Turgeau house. We drove for what seemed like an eternity but was probably less than ten minutes. Colton pulled off the road again, this time onto something soft that made shushing sounds against the tires. He didn't retrieve me immediately, and the waiting almost drove me crazy. By the time the trunk cracked open, sweat covered my body and I gasped for air.

My first good look at Colton scared me even more. Tears streaked his face, but intense purpose burned in his eyes. That alone inspired me to scream behind my gag. I paused for breath, and he picked that moment to speak.

"You'll pass out if you keep on," he said. "But that might make dying easier."

Everything stopped. My shoulders sagged. I didn't resist much as he pulled me out of the car, removed his belt, and bound my hands in front of me with duct tape. Belatedly, I began to fight when he tried to loop a dog leash around my neck. I ducked out of his reach. "I don't want to kill you, but you and Lisette are the two nosiest bitches I've ever seen."

Lisette? What did she have to do with this? Julienne banished her from the house.

Colton struck while I thought things over, grabbing me by the neck and slipping the dog leash over my head. He jerked it, trying to lead me away from the car. I dug my heels into the dirt and locked my knees. Colton pulled again and the looped leash tightened around my neck, choking off my air supply. A pressure and a spookily reassuring darkness built behind my eyes. It hit me that I might not want to let Colton choke me into unconsciousness. If I passed out, I wouldn't have any chance of fighting my way out of this. The next time he jerked the leash, I followed.

He led me into a clearing looking out on a murky, slime-covered pond. A long pier stretched out onto the water. A figure sat tied to a pylon. We drew closer, and I recognized Lisette. My imagination ran wild. I tried to push thoughts of what Colton had planned out of my mind. If I let them enter, I'd panic. If I panicked, I'd have no chance of getting out of here. So I focused on Lisette.

Could there be any more horrible way to die than with my boyfriend's ex-wife? I half-heartedly considered asking Colton to go ahead and kill me so I wouldn't have to suffer her company for even a minute. Then our eyes locked. Rather than her usual arrogance, I saw fear...and something else I could work with: anger.

COLTON LED me to a spot next to her and forced me to a kneeling position. I made myself hold still. Fighting would only convince him I needed to be further restrained. More restraints meant less chance I'd see the next day. He duct taped me to the same post, back to back with Lisette.

Lisette spoke behind her duct tape gag. Colton tensed, his movements becoming jerky. Realizing what bothered him, I began to scream behind my hanky gag. Colton stood and shook his fist at us.

"Y'all stop that. Nobody's going to hear you back here. We're acres away from the house and the workers."

Knowing I was onto something, I closed my eyes and screamed through my nose. Behind me, Lisette started up. Colton clenched his fists and grimaced.

"Stop it. Stop it. Stop it." He yelled louder than both of us put together. We kept on screaming, only pausing to gather more air. Colton dropped to his knees in front of us. "If I take out your gag, will you stop?"

I nodded, and he pulled the disgusting hanky out of my mouth. He held one finger to his lips for me to be quiet. I nodded. At least I could breathe. He went through the same routine with Lisette. Of course, she started talking as soon as the tape was off her mouth.

"You sorry bastard." Then to my amazement, Lisette

pitched her voice in a whisper, as though that would keep Colton, who bent over us, from hearing, "Come on. Do something. You act like you get into fights all the time."

This had to be a nightmare. Surely, I'd wake soon, perhaps in the afterlife. Anything would be better than this.

To Lisette, I said, "Yeah. I whup people's asses all the time when my hands are duct taped together."

Colton chuckled. "Peri Jean, I am really sorry it has come to this. I think we could have been great friends."

"You know, if you hadn't kidnapped me, I wouldn't have suspected you," I said. He sighed, sat down on a cinderblock, and took out his switchblade.

"That's bullshit. I saw it on your face. Lisette here figured it out too. She can place me in Houston the summer after Shayne's disappearance."

Lisette figured it out before me? Now I really want to die.

"Houston is where I bought the ring." She paused and shifted against my back. The duct tape binding us together tightened, and pins and needles tingled in my fingertips. "When I confronted him today, he cried like a little bitch."

I wished I could kick her. She had no reason to crow. She was about to die over her stupidity.

"Why didn't you tell the sheriff's office back then?" I moaned the words, not really expecting any answer from Lisette. But she wasn't one to take a rebuke in silence.

"Because it never hit me then. I never put the two together." She said it like I should have known, the same way she'd have told me water was wet. And I guess that's how it played out in her mind. Lisette saw what she wanted and ignored what she didn't want in every situation.

"So you confronted this idiot by yourself after you knew he murdered Shayne?" I twisted as far as I could, trying to look at her. "How have you lived this long, Lisette?"

"You shut up." She cried a few half-hearted sobs. They sounded more like frustration than genuine remorse. "I didn't think Colton could do anything like that. That summer, after Shayne died, he was in Houston, taking graduate classes. I called him. We went out. We—"

I closed my eyes and made a disgusted sound. Not only would I die with Dean's ex-wife, I'd die with Dean's trampy ex-wife. I faced forward again. I didn't want to see Lisette, to see the person who cheated on Dean with strangers, with their teacher, and who knew who else.

COLTON RIPPED a strip of duct tape off the roll and pushed it over Lisette's mouth. "That's enough. You've reminded me of that afternoon too many times over the years, and I'd just as soon forget it. You laid there like a fish. It wasn't anything worth remembering."

Had I not been about to die, I'd have smiled. Then he ripped another strip of duct tape off the roll and pushed it down on my lips. I squealed in protest.

"I've been thinking of the most painless way to do this, girls."

Girls? I cursed at him behind my tape.

"I think the quickest way is blunt force trauma to the head." He picked up a posthole digger, gripping it as though testing its heft. "You'll only feel a flash of pain. I'll weight you down with those cinderblocks." He pointed. "And I'll dispose of you in the pond. Even if you aren't quite dead, you'll drown before you wake up."

My heart stuttered. Cold sweat broke out over my body. I had a hard time sucking oxygen through my nose. Imagining myself at the bottom of the pond, fright overtook me. The world around me seemed distant. I couldn't follow any one train of thought. Colton mistook the look on my face as a signal I wanted to talk more.

"I made a mistake with poor Shayne, trying to strangle her." He shuddered as he remembered. Then anger flashed over his face, transforming his features into twisted evil. "Shayne didn't understand why I needed top billing on the *Disappearing Culture* project. I'd have never gotten grants for graduate school without that."

Lisette mumbled some words at him from behind her gag.

"You don't understand, 'Sette." He dropped the posthole digger on the pier and approached us, squatting on one of his cinder blocks. "You've had every advantage money can buy. My sister and I grew up orphans, shuffled from one relative to another. The only way I could go to college was with a scholarship. I dreamed of having a great job where I earned enough money to not have to depend on others." He held out his hands, palms up, like he was giving a speech at Toastmasters.

Though grateful for the reprieve of execution, I didn't

understand why he needed to justify his behavior. He planned to kill us. Did he care what we thought? *What a weirdo.* At least every moment he talked gave me another few seconds to think of a way to get out of this.

"That project—*Disappearing Culture*—was my ticket out of teaching high school English and into teaching college-level folklore." He gave us a smile. "But Shayne wanted credit for the interviews. I couldn't do that. What if it hurt me in grad school? She figured out I sold some school property. I needed that money for grad school. She tried to blackmail me. And, of course, she'd figured out I stole those stupid fucking coins. So that was it." Colton stopped speaking, staring out into the distance, lost in thought, probably working up to killing us. "Shayne never understood we all sometimes have to sacrifice for the greater good of others."

Underneath my terror, my anger brewed. I hated people who thought the world owed them something. Yes, Colton's early life sounded hardscrabble. He worked hard to pull himself out of it. And I respected that. But he shat all over his accomplishments by cheating, stealing, and murdering to tip the scales in his favor. Colton, despite his physical beauty, was a disgusting troll of a human being.

I squeezed my eyes shut and tried to figure out a way to live through this. Thoughts swirled around, none of them making any sense, and Lisette blubbered behind me. I was well and truly stuck. Then I sensed a shift in the air, the kind ghosts usually cause. For once in my sorry life, I was thankful for what I was.

A BOARD CREAKING snapped me out of my reverie, and I cracked my eyes open to see Colton put his face in his hands. He whispered to himself, but I couldn't hear the words over the roaring in my head.

Out of the corner of my eye, I glimpsed flashes of Shayne's ghost as she moved along the banks of the pond. It seemed she wanted to help but didn't know how.

She materialized next to Colton and tapped his shoulder. He jumped and looked around him, trying to figure out what had touched him. Shayne materialized next to Lisette and me. She reached out one translucent hand and caressed my cheek. Her frigid touch burned, and I jerked away. She was my last hope, but we hadn't communicated very well thus far. I decided to try again.

I conjured a picture of Dean, the only person who could save us at this point, and pushed the image at Shayne. She continued flickering in and out of visibility in the clearing. I begged her to help us as hard as I could, but she remained unaffected. Calling up every bit of energy I had, I pushed it at Shayne. She whipped around to stare at me, her eyes black holes, and disappeared. *Shit. I ran her off.*

Colton picked that moment to grow a pair. He stood and walked over to where he'd dropped the posthole digger and took it up again. He walked slowly toward us, practicing his swing. If he carried out his plan, Lisette and I would pay for his lack of skill. I suspected it would take several blows for him to kill us. My legs jumped and trembled on their own accord.

Something pressed against my hand, and I jumped. Shayne's cold fingers curled around my wrist and pressed the item into my hand again. By this time, I recognized the feel of Fayette's crazy necklace. I closed my fingers around it, feeling the zing of power shoot up my arm. I gave myself to it, closing my eyes with the effort.

I felt myself rising, floating upwards and out of my body. I cracked my eyes and looked down at the scene below us. Everything seemed so clear up here. I couldn't hear Colton's thoughts, but I sensed them in a weird way.

Colton didn't want to kill us, but he'd already killed Trey and Shayne to preserve what he'd worked so hard to achieve. Why not two more? Besides, Lisette would one day spill the beans about the afternoon they spent doing the naked monkey dance when she was still a teenager and he a grown man. That would be embarrassing and possibly ruin his relationship with the Turgeau family.

Lisette didn't want to die and was scared. But she also worried about how she'd look when her body was found. She wondered if Dean would be sorry now for not taking her back. She hated she had to die with me.

Feeling's mutual, sister.

Shayne stood at the end of the pier near a clump of saw palmettos, her head tilted at the sky watching me. Had this been all she could do for me? Get me out of my body so I wouldn't have to be present while Colton bashed in my head and drowned me? Shayne's exasperated thoughts reached me, still a hiss of unintelligible whispers. I concentrated harder, focusing on the power of the necklace and heard "snake."

I jerked in midair, looking for the offending creature, worried it might bite me. I felt Shayne trying to get my attention. I glanced her way. She pointed at a spot on the ground next to her. I zeroed in on it and, for the first time, knew what I had to do.

When I got close to the snake, it raised its triangular head and its fat body shifted into a coil. The familiar odor of its musk filled the air. A water moccasin. Even though I didn't feel my body, I still felt goose bumps rise all over me. The snake flicked its pink tongue out at me and drew back its head to strike. How would I get it over to Colton?

I rushed at the snake and it struck, its jaw unhinging to display that white mouth for which its breed is known. *It can see me.* A second later, it struck again. But, since I was not corporeal at the moment, it hit nothing and tried to crawl away from me, confused. I herded the poor animal down the pier toward Colton and Lisette. I risked having it strike her, but I was out of options. Turned out, Lisette and Colton did the heavy lifting for me.

Lisette saw the snake wriggling toward her. Her eyes widened in terror. Colton, seeing her response directed at something behind him, turned. When he saw the thick, black snake coming at him, he screamed and tried to strike it with the posthole digger. I'd been correct about his level of skill with the thing. The snake dodged the shovel with no problem. Though water moccasins were not aggressive snakes, it was scared and it struck Colton's leg.

I don't know if the fangs connected with his skin that

time, but they sure did when Colton reached down to grab the snake and pull it off him. The handsome man threw back his head and screamed, cords standing out on his neck. The snake struck again.

I slid back into my body and leaned away from the post Colton had taped us to with all my might. The tape stretched, pulling against Lisette. She squealed at first, but quickly caught on.

The two of us pulled the tape, using our sit-up muscles. Between the sweat and Colton's piss poor job of securing us, we loosened it enough to slip from under it. I peeled the duct tape from my face and went to Lisette, peeled off her gag, and picked at the end of the tape binding her hands until I could start it unraveling. From there, it went fast. Soon, her hands were free. She shoved around me, nearly knocking me into water, and took off running, screaming for Dean.

I glanced back at Colton. The snake had crawled off to live another day. Colton lay on his side on the wide part of the pier, shivering. If he didn't get medical attention soon, I doubted he'd survive the attack. If he died, I'd be responsible. Part of me thought I should help him, but he tried to kill me, dammit. I took off running, broke out of the woods, and almost collapsed with relief.

Dean and Ricky sped across the field in the utility vehicle they'd been using for their work. Nadine sat in the backseat. She stood and pointed, slapping Ricky, who was driving, on the shoulder until he saw Lisette and me straggling toward him. Lisette continued screaming and running until she reached the utility vehicle. I slowed to a walk. The whole thing was done, and I was just about too tired to take another step.

From a short distance away, I watched Lisette throw herself on Dean, sobbing on his shoulder. She glanced at me approaching, her eyes glittering with a mean twinkle I'd learned to recognize over the past couple of days.

"Get the hell away from me." Dean shoved Lisette off him and ran to me. He hugged me to him, squeezing until I thought my bones would break. Finally, he let me loose and held me where he could look at me. I could have stayed in his arms a little longer.

"How'd she get untied?" He gestured at Lisette who was busy crawling all over Ricky.

"I did it." I didn't add that she ran off and left me once I'd helped her, but Dean understood and rolled his eyes as he unwrapped my wrists.

"Where's Colton? When we couldn't find you, Nadine told me and Ricky you had to be with him."

"Back there on the pier. He got snake bit." I paused, trying to figure out how to say the next part. Finally, I just said it. "He killed her, Dean. Colton killed Shayne."

Dean's face drained of color. He glanced at Ricky patting Lisette's back while she wailed. Taking out his cell phone, he called emergency services. His voice trembled as he explained the kind of help we needed. When he finished, I knew I needed to tell him why Colton killed Shayne. It hurt to say the words.

"He killed her because he wanted all the credit for the *Disappearing Culture* books. Shayne got angry at the unfairness of it and threatened to blow the whistle on him for selling school property." Dean and Ricky both stared at me, gape-mouthed. "Colton also stole Trey's coin collection. The coin with Shayne's body was an attempt to frame Trey." I didn't tell them Colton killed Trey because I had no way of explaining how I knew.

Dean wept over the unfairness of it. While I held him, Shayne's ghost passed us, moving toward the house. She acknowledged me with a nod and a wash of grateful emotion. I watched her walk across the field, expecting her to move on to the next plane of existence, but realized she didn't want to move on. She would remain in her family home, haunting future generations of Turgeaus.

17

The next morning, Dean and I packed his BMW while the sun was still new and dew sparkled in the grass. An ambulance would bring his father home later that day, and Julienne recommended we leave before then. She said Dean's father would think of a reason we needed to stay.

My father's vintage Nova would be restored to its former glory and towed to Gaslight City—a gift from Ricky Turgeau for solving his sister's murder. He felt terrible for choosing such a creep for a best friend. I just told him, "We all trust the wrong person at one time or another."

The St. Namadie Parish Sheriff's Office closed the case the day before. Colton confessed to everything from his hospital bed. Sheriff Braezeale said he suspected Colton would take a plea bargain to avoid the death penalty.

As Dean closed the trunk, his mother hustled out to the car carrying something in her hand. When she got closer, I saw she grasped a linen hanky. I hoped she brought us some of the wonderful blueberry muffins her cook made us for breakfast. To my disappointment, I saw whatever she held was too small to be a muffin.

Speaking to Dean, she said, "Your baby sister wants to play the piano and sing for you before you go."

After a long look exchanged with his mother, Dean nodded and headed into the house without argument.

What's this all about?

"I want you to have this." She handed me the handkerchief.

I took it and opened it. Inside was Fayette's necklace. The same little buzz of magic I'd always felt from it tickled my hand. I tried to hand it back. "I can't take this. It belongs in your family."

"You can. My grandmother left it to me in her will with very specific instructions. She said to enjoy it, but to pass it along to the right person. She said I'd know when I met them. And I did." Julienne smiled.

I thought about the way the necklace had followed me around since I arrived here. It might follow me home whether I accepted it or not. And a flutter of intuition told me I might need it sometime.

"Fayette left a note in her will for me to relate to the recipient. Are you ready?"

I nodded.

"It magnifies whatever you are."

My stomach twisted. I didn't know quite what to feel about that. It explained my hearing the ghost's voices when I wore it. Nice to know I could possibly shut them off, too, at least. But I wondered what kind of trouble this necklace could get me into...or out of, for that matter.

"It's beautiful. Thank you." I slipped the long chain over my head and had a flash of the woman who'd owned it before me standing right next to Julienne. She disappeared as quickly as she appeared. *I'll have to be careful with this thing. That's for sure.*

Julienne glanced back at the house and then at me. "If you ever need anything, no matter what happens between you and Dean, know that you can come see me. I will help you any way I can."

I wasn't sure how to react, and Julienne didn't seem to expect me to. She began speaking again, her words hurried.

"My son cares for you. I'd have to be blind and deaf not to recognize that, but I also know how he is, how he needs to save people. I'm not sure you need saving." She smiled and leaned forward. "Matter of fact, you might end up saving him. Am I right?"

I shrugged and smiled.

"I hope he can get over himself enough to see the treasure he's got. But, no matter what happens, you are one of us now."

Emotion swelled in my chest, and tears burned my eyes. Although Colton had been a monster, he'd been right about one thing. This family took in people. *No wonder Lisette kept coming around.* I felt grateful to know them. Julienne and I hugged.

"Before he comes back, can I ask you something?" I glanced at the house's huge front door, relieved to find it still closed.

Julienne nodded.

"Why is he so uncomfortable with what I am?" I'd made up my mind to accept Dean not loving this part of me. But I needed to understand it, especially after learning of Fayette.

Julienne scrunched up her face while she thought. "Fayette was old and sick by the time Dean knew her. Her judgment of what it is appropriate to tell a little boy, especially one as serious as Dean, had gone bad. Right before she died, she told him no matter how hard he tried to protect his sister, he wouldn't be able to."

Cold chills danced over my skin, making me shiver despite the hot morning. No wonder I scared Dean. Where Fayette had the power to tell him things he didn't want to hear, I could make him see things he didn't want to see. I didn't blame Dean for being scared of me. I scared myself, but I wanted to learn to be me comfortably.

Dean and Madeleine came out of the house munching on blueberry muffins. They slapped and kicked at each other as they walked toward us, both of them grinning and giggling. Madeleine pulled me into a tight hug and shoved a croissant into my hand. I wanted to laugh. *This family and their food. They could make a reality show on the dysfunction.*

"Come back soon," she said.

"You come see me in Gaslight City," I told her. "Meet my grandmother. She'd get a kick out of you."

Madeleine said she would, and Julienne hugged me one more time. Dean opened the BMW's door for me, and I slid in. Julienne leaned into the car, kissed me on the cheek, whispered in my ear, "Come back soon. I can't wait to get to know you better."

A dark cloud settled over me despite Julienne's kindness. Being an honorary member of her family didn't take away the sting of how little family I had left. Once Memaw died, I'd have nobody who shared my genes. Just an uncle serving life in prison who refused to see me. I wondered again about Memaw's family, the Gregsons. They shared my ability. Memaw all but forbade me to make contact with them. But I wanted to know them. I wanted a family like this one, one who always opened their arms and loved me just because.

Then I thought about Colton. Unsatisfied with the life he earned, he cheated his way into another one. He stole Shayne's life. He stole her family. But it caught up with him and destroyed him. I made up my mind to cherish Julienne's friendship, but to never forget where I came from and who I was.

Dean started the car and pulled away from the house. In the rearview mirror, it looked like something out of a TV show. But now I knew the truth. Good people lived there who had problems just as bad as mine. Julienne waved to us as we drove up the driveway. We pulled onto the road, and Dean turned on the stereo. Classic rock on a satellite station in a BMW. The clash between the two made me smile.

"Let's go home." Dean held out his hand over the console. I took it and twined my fingers through his. We drove down the narrow asphalt road where I first saw Shayne and turned on to the main highway. I leaned back in the seat and relaxed as we sped up. The last three days seemed like an eternity. I felt like I could sleep a week and still feel tired.

Through half-closed eyes, I spotted a figure walking alongside the road. The shaggy blond hair hanging over his collar and the guitar slung over his back reminded me of a friend of mine, one who no longer walked the earth because of decisions I made. We passed the man, and I twisted in my seat to keep him in my sightline. He raised his head. The features were wrong. Face too thin. Lips too full. He was somebody else altogether. That other man was a memory I still held, one difficult to release. I glanced over at Dean.

We didn't have much history, and he didn't love everything about me. But he was willing to try hard to make it work. Whatever I did, whatever I chose, it was all on me.

Dean and I sped toward the future. I didn't think I was ready, but time waits for nobody.

Keep reading for an excerpt of
the next
Peri Jean Mace Ghost Thriller.

ROCKS & GRAVEL (EXCERPT)

PERI JEAN MACE GHOST THRILLERS #3

I ran up the museum steps, breathing hard, sweat running down the back of my neck. The August humidity pushed at me like a wet, invisible wall. Every step was an effort. My heart pounded both from the strain on my cigarette-singed lungs and the shock of Hannah's phone call. *Get here, now. I need you.* I stopped to stare at the poster mounted in the museum's plate glass window. It featured a picture of a guy who could have been a movie star and read:

DEPUTY DEAN FOR SHERIFF
NEW BLOOD
NEW IDEAS
THE RIGHT MAN FOR THE JOB

I bet my last pair of clean undies this poster and the guy in the picture—who happened to be my boyfriend—were the problem. If someone in Hannah's family just saw it, they probably got all butt hurt she wasn't supporting her uncle, the incumbent sheriff. I took a deep breath and raised my hand to knock on the door. It swung open before my fist made contact.

"Peri Jean Mace, what are you doing out there? Playing with yourself? Get on in here." Tear tracks striped Hannah's freckled cheeks, and her wildly patterned kimono hung limp around her legs. I couldn't believe she wasn't even dressed yet.

She grabbed my arm and jerked me into the museum's foyer. Then she leaned out the door and peered up and down the misty streets, empty at this early hour. Satisfied nobody was there, she closed the door and locked it. She grabbed her oversized coffee mug from the reception desk and lifted it to her lips, hand trembling so badly she almost spilled coffee on herself. She set it back down and closed her eyes.

I dug for my cigarettes but stopped when I remembered she wouldn't let me smoke inside. The clock at the Catholic church a block away chimed seven times, reminding me I got less than three hours sleep the night before. Caring for my terminally ill grandmother was a twenty-four-hour job with no sick days. Adrenaline would keep me moving for a little while longer but not much.

"Take the poster down if they're upset over it. Dean'll understand." Acknowledging how tired I felt had been a mistake. I wanted nothing more than to crash on Hannah's couch for a half hour. If I wrapped up her problem right away, I could grab a half hour of sleep before my first job of the day started.

"Huh?" The upset drained off her face, replaced by

confusion. "What are you talking about? The campaign sign? Oh, they're mad, but they weren't speaking to me anyway, so they can pound sand."

"Then what on earth has you calling me over here at the ass crack of dawn?" I pushed past her, followed the scent of coffee to her office, and poured myself a cup, still holding onto the hope this problem could be solved with a few wise words. Maybe she'd figured out one of her silly, interchangeable boyfriends had a wife stowed somewhere.

"Someone broke into my safe last night and stole some..." She glanced around her office as though the thief might have left a listening device and delivered the last part of her announcement in a loud whisper. "Some really important stuff belonging to the Bruce family."

I nearly dropped my coffee. Once I got over my surprise, the disappointment set in. There was no way I'd get a nap. Hooty's family heirlooms getting stolen, especially while Hannah had possession of them, constituted tears, tantrums, and anything else Hannah could think of to do. I groaned and sat down in my usual chair next to the window and fought against the fatigue gumming up my brain.

"What got stolen?"

"Some old journals. A book on folk medicine." Hannah sat behind her desk and began twisting her fingers. I wanted to tell her if she didn't quit pulling on them they'd get as long as octopus tentacles. "Irreplaceable. There aren't even copies."

"Who'd care enough about those to steal them?"

"Both were connected to the Mace Treasure."

I closed my eyes and rubbed the bridge of my nose. She didn't need to say more. Damn it all to hell and back. I hated the Mace Treasure. I hated the people who ran around like jackasses hunting for it. I bit my lower lip, wishing I could tell Hannah I had to leave, any excuse would do. *Suck it up, Peri Jean Mace*, said my inner adult. I sat up straight, still thinking maybe there was a way I could extract myself from the craziness.

"I saw Rainey's car in front of her law office when I passed through town. Want me to call her?" I knew Rainey Bruce would shout at me. She'd been doing it since we were in kindergarten. Her father might act nicer, but I hated to call him this early. "Hooty's probably still at home. I didn't see his car in front of the funeral home."

"Hell, no. I don't want you to call them. Do you know how this is going to look? They're important people here in town. Everybody at Hooty's church is going to know, and—and—and…" Hannah's face crumpled, and she lowered her head.

I let her cry for a few seconds. "Okay. Enough boo-hooing. We have to get on top of this. Have you called in the theft? Let the sheriff's office do their thing?"

"Uncle Joey's not speaking to me. I can't talk to him." She said it with such finality I knew there had to be a long, juicy story. Another time.

"Call Dean directly. He can get the wheels rolling." Truth was, if Dean figured out Hannah called me instead of reporting the theft, he'd be hurt and angry. Probably at both of us for not trusting his ability to do his job.

She stared at me, face long and sad, still tugging on her

fingers. My Something-Is-Wrong detector went on red alert.

"I'm not sure Dean can help." She sounded like a little girl asking an adult if she could use the restroom. "But I think you can."

Oh, no. If Dean couldn't help, but I could, it could only be one thing.

Ghosts.

It was too damn early in the morning for ghosts. What's more, I didn't want the trouble they brought into my life. Things were stressful enough between caring for my sick memaw and my boyfriend running for sheriff. I sat back in my chair, fighting against the stress headache starting in the back of my neck.

"What haven't you told me?"

"Maybe I'd better show you."

Some days, hiding in a hole would be preferable to facing the world. This was turning out to be one of those days. I sucked down the last of my coffee and set my cup aside.

Hannah clicked some keys on her laptop and motioned to me. "Come over here so you can see, too." I obeyed but not happily. She tapped a key, and a grainy picture of her empty office popped onto the screen. A shadow crossed the room, and my heart jittered. I leaned closer to the screen, not wanting to see but unable to help myself. The shadow moved to a picture on the wall and hovered there for several moments. A stack of books drifted from the wall and floated across the room.

"Holy stinking socks." I'd never seen a ghost move

items, especially substantial ones, very far. "But how did the books get in the wall behind the painting?"

"New safe. Installed last month at the insistence of the museum board. Apparently, this one isn't secure." Hannah gestured at the huge, cast iron safe behind her desk.

"Those clever little tricksters. Gonna tell them the theft probably wouldn't have happened if the items had been in the iron safe?"

She shook her head and stared at me, waiting for me to say something, but I was too full of fatigue to pick up on what she wanted. "So was the shadow on the video a ghost?"

"I guess." I stared longingly at the coffeemaker. I wanted another cup, but the acid in my stomach wouldn't allow it.

"You don't know? You've seen ghosts your whole life and don't know?" Her voice rose with each word. "I want you to wear your black opal necklace and watch it again."

She spun around in her chair and fiddled with the door to the cast iron safe.

"I don't know." I put one hand on my churning stomach. "I sort of promised Dean to keep the woo-woo stuff on the down low until the sheriff's election ended."

"You won't help me?" Angry red, which matched Hannah's hair color, bloomed on her cheekbones. "Because your boyfriend's scared of what you can do?"

My cheeks grew warm, and I fought to keep my calm. I did not want to start the day fighting with my best friend.

Hannah glared at me across the desk. The glare itself didn't bother me. Her hissy fits changed as often as the

East Texas weather. The pure hurt behind her anger, however, chipped at my heart. *Maybe I should help.*

"I'll do it on one condition."

"What's the condition?"

"The black opal goes back in your cast iron safe when I'm done."

"Agreed." She opened the safe, took out a velvet pouch, and set it on the desk between us. The pouch's contents formed a small lump. As we watched, the lump moved and then disappeared altogether. I felt the weight of the black opal around my neck. Hannah gasped.

"It truly does freak me out when it does that," she said.

"Yeah. Imagine how I feel." My nervous system felt like it was lined with ground glass. "Play the video again."

She did. The black opal lent me a little extra ghost vision, giving the shadow a more human form. Between the lighting and the video's low quality, I couldn't make out much detail. Broad shoulders and narrow hips tipped me to the ghost's sex.

"I think it's a man, but I can't see his face yet." The books floated out of the safe, only this time, I could see two ghostly hands holding them. The ghost turned to leave the room and faced the camera. His face was fuzzy with dark hollows for eyes and a blur where the nose and mouth were, but I saw nothing identifying. I was ready to give up, but I heard something.

"Stop the video."

Hannah scrambled to do what I asked.

"Do you have headphones? Loud ones?"

She dug in her desk and got out a set of bright green

headphones and plugged them into the laptop. She rewound the video, and I turned up the volume as loud as it would go, wincing at the hiss bombarding my eardrums.

"Don't want to do this," said a garbled, tiny voice.

The hair on the back of my neck stood up. I leaned closer to the screen as though it would help me hear better.

"My friends. Can't do this." The books came out of the wall. The shadow turned to face the camera. "Please make it stop."

I jerked away from the computer, knocked into Hannah, and pulled the headphones off my head. My skin stung as every nerve ending in my body tried to short circuit and burn out. I tossed the headphones into Hannah's lap.

"What was it?"

I shook my head and took out my cigarettes, lighting one with shaking hands and turning my back on Hannah's protests. She restarted the video and put on the headphones. When it finished she took them off and shook her head. "Your face is green. You look ready to spew puke all over my office. And you're stinking this place up with your awful cigarettes. Please tell me what you heard."

The pleading in the ghost's voice bothered me, but something else did, too. Something deep in my brain where I couldn't quite access it. I squashed out my cigarette in my empty coffee cup.

"What is it?" Hannah grabbed my arm and gave it a shake. "Please."

"Whatever we saw on the video didn't want to be there. It was forced. Someone, somewhere, is controlling it."

Hannah and I stared at each other, both of us breathing hard.

"So if I find who's controlling the ghost—"

"You find your thief." I might have said more, but I heard running footsteps on the street outside. I got up and peered out the window. "There's Dean on his morning run. Let's tell him what's happened. He can at least alert local antique dealers and pawn shops to be on the lookout. If someone stole the items to sell, you might get them back." I tapped on the window to get his attention. My muscles tensed while I waited for him to turn around. These days, I never knew which Dean I'd get. The sweet, reasonable one or the one this election changed into a crotchety old grouch who could turn petty and mean over a popcorn fart.

Dean turned and smiled at me. I smiled back and motioned him inside. Shoulders relaxing, I went to the door and let him inside. This election couldn't be over soon enough. Dean's moodiness wore me out worse than a hard day's work. I wanted us to start having fun together again.

"Hey, gorgeous." His kiss almost made me forget the weird feeling I had about all this. "Missed you last night. Your memaw okay?"

"Sleeping when I left." She was dying of cancer, and I was overwhelmed. Not much help for either problem. "Got something job related for you. Hannah's had a theft."

A few minutes later, Dean sat in Hannah's office chair

—which she'd insisted on covering with a towel so his sweat wouldn't get on it—watching the video.

"Somebody tampered with your system, but I don't understand how." He restarted the video and watched with his face close to the screen. "I know an expert in Houston, but who knows how long it'll take him or if he can figure out who did it. I'm not even completely sure Burns County can afford him."

Hannah and I exchanged a glance. Frustration brewed in her caramel eyes, taking them from warm to hot. Dean's reaction didn't surprise me, either. Hannah needed to understand we were at a dead end.

"My first job of the day starts in less than ten minutes," I said. Dean rose to kiss me but sat right back down to replay the video for the umpteenth time.

"I'll walk you out." Hannah followed close at my heels, not speaking until we reached my car. I opened the door, pretending I thought we'd said all we had to say to each other.

"Dean can't help, and you know it." She leaned into my face. "If you think I'm going to let you walk away from this because you're afraid—"

"I'm not afraid." I took off the black opal necklace and held it out to her. "Don't let Dean see this, please." She took it, dropped it into her pocket, and fixed me with a dirty look.

"Soon as I said the stolen items had to do with the Mace Treasure, you got this tightassed expression on your face and started doing the pee-pee dance. But okay. You're not afraid."

I opened my mouth to argue, but the sound of several loud motorcycles drowned me out. Hannah and I stopped talking to watch them come.

"What are the Six Gun Revolutionaries doing here?" Hannah yelled at me. I shrugged. She stepped back from the curb and glanced toward the museum, probably looking for Dean. I hoped he didn't hear the ruckus but knew there was no way he could miss it.

The convoy of motorcycles slowed and pulled up next to the curb, surrounding my car. It was then I saw who they had with them. King Tolliver, the president of the motorcycle club, had attached a matching sidecar to his bright blue Harley Davidson. Sitting in it, goggles on her face and a bandana covering her hair was Memaw. *Oh, hell no.* I marched over to her.

"What on earth are you doing?" I had to yell to hear over the motorcycles. She shook her head. Furious, I screamed, "Shut these loud-assed road mongers off."

Nobody did anything until King cut off his motorcycle. He gave me a lizard-eyed stare.

"What are you doing?" I studied Memaw for signs the cancer had spread to her brain. I could think of no other reason for her to be associating with these outlaws.

"Calm down." Like magic, Wade Hill appeared at my side to tower over me. He draped one heavy arm over my shoulders. I shrugged him off. We worked together at least once a week for my odd jobs business. I knew his ways, and I wouldn't let him soft shoe me.

"This is on my bucket list." Memaw grinned wider than

I'd seen on a long time. "I wanted to ride with a real badass biker gang. Just like on TV."

"This isn't TV. It's going to be a hundred degrees by noon. It's already hellish out here." To prove my point, I pulled my already damp t-shirt off my skin.

"That's why we started early," Memaw said. "I'm gonna have a fried chicken lunch for them as thanks."

"See?" Wade tried putting his arm over my shoulders again. I tried to shrug him off, but he didn't budge. He tugged me away from Memaw and walked me a short distance away. He spoke in a low voice. "She's running out of time. Let her enjoy herself without giving her shit."

My first impulse was to tell him Memaw wasn't running out of time, but I knew she was, which infuriated me. I wanted to argue, to tell him she needed to take care of herself, but I knew it didn't matter. The end would be the same. I nodded to let Wade know I understood and squeezed his huge arm in thanks. He gave me a rough back pat, nearly knocking me off my feet. I walked to Memaw and gave her a hug.

"Enjoy," I told her. To King, I said, "Make her drink water." He gave me the same lizard stare but winked to let me know he understood. He started up his motorcycle, and the rest of his club followed suit. I waved as they drove away, feeling as though I'd lost something, but I didn't know what.

I turned to find Hannah and Dean whispering together on the museum steps and glancing at me. I got into my car and hightailed it out of there before they decided to include me in their conversation.

I chain-smoked my way to the first job of the day, trying every trick I knew to forget the creepy figure in the surveillance video. I needed to forget the theft and go about my business. Nothing concerning the Mace Treasure had any place in my life, ghosts or no ghosts.

Those awful, pleading words wouldn't leave me. *Don't want to do this. My friends. Can't do this.* Then the most awful part, when the ghost faced the camera as though he somehow knew I'd watch this video. *Please make it stop.*

The same sense of déjà vu I had at the museum crept over me. Somehow I should know this voice, but I didn't. A familiar weight settled around my neck, and I almost dropped my cigarette in my lap trying to feel what it was. *The black opal. Could this day possibly get worse?* I wondered how the piece of jewelry got away from Hannah before she had time to put it up.

Dean's mother gave me the black opal because of what I am. It originally belonged to Dean's great-grandmother, who had what some folks call the Sight. The black opal had serious power. Aside from following me around like an overzealous dog, the gem's magical properties increased my ability to see ghosts and communicate with them. If I spent all day every day farting around with woo-woo, the black opal would have helped me immensely. But I did my best to stay away from magical stuff.

Amanda's Hair Flair, my first job of the day, came up on the right. I turned into the parking lot but stayed in my car to finish my cigarette. Time to put on my game face.

Running a business required me to act competent. Business aside, I didn't want to revive the town rumor about my lack of sanity. A spring in the backseat creaked. The car shifted. I glanced into the rearview mirror and screamed.

A shadowy figure sat in my backseat. The voice came to me again, the black opal vibrating with the words. *Please make it stop.*

I grabbed for the door handle, fingers slipping off in my eagerness to get away from this thing. It had power, power enough to take a pile of books out of the library. What could it do to me? I swung open the door and found myself face to face with my mother. I screamed again.

"What do you think, honey?" She finger-fluffed her hair. Her grin would have put a shit-eating possum's to shame.

Didn't she hear me scream? It expressed exactly what I thought about her and her hair. Seeing her reactivated the acidic coffee in my stomach, and I clutched my middle. *What on earth was she doing in town?*

"Amanda told me you were scheduled to help her today, and I just had to see my baby girl." She made a shrill sound likely meant as a combination giggle and squeal and grabbed me in a hug I didn't want. The little girl who lived deep in my psyche, the one who still ached for her mother's love, forced me to half-assedly return the hug. It was enough for Barbie. She dropped her arms immediately. "Last time I saw you, your hair was in one of those sleek, short styles. Looked good. You've got your daddy's hair, you know."

"I saw some old pictures of myself. Thought it was time

for a change." I picked at my nails, which looked awful, so I wouldn't have to make eye contact with Barbie and waited for her to say something so I could formulate a response. I wanted to run away from her, get in my car, and leave, but Memaw raised me to act better. She raised me to treat people with respect, even the ones who deserved to have roach doo doo rubbed on their faces.

"Might look good if you can get past the stage it's at now." She snorted. "I cut mine short when I was about ten years older than you. Tried to grow it out a dozen times and never made it."

The back of my neck began to throb from me clenching my shoulder muscles. I had no idea how to communicate with the woman who gave me life, nor any desire to learn. Amanda joined us with a bottle of one of her homemade beauty potions in hand.

"I am so glad you are back in town to stay." She drew Barbie into a one-armed hug and gave her a loud kiss on the cheek. She turned to me and pulled me into the hug. I stiffened, but Amanda was stronger than I could have imagined. Resisting her would have been noticeable, and I never aired dirty family laundry in public. "Ain't you glad your momma's gonna be living near you again?"

"You can't imagine," I mumbled. A buzz filled my head. *Back in town to stay?* It made no sense. "W-w-w-" *Pull it together, Peri Jean,* I instructed myself and started again. "What made you decide to move back here?"

"You mean back to a one-horse town?" Barbie threw back her head and laughed. "Back to everything I couldn't wait to get away from when I was twenty-five?" She stared at me for too long and pressed her lips together. "Mostly you. I missed you." She threw her arms around me again.

The reek of her perfume cloaked me, and I felt my gorge rising. The buzz in my head got so loud it made me dizzy. I willed my knees not to buckle. Barbie released me so she could stare into my face. I couldn't meet her gaze.

"Amanda said you're dating the guy who's running for sheriff. I saw his campaign poster. What a hottie." She rubbed my arms as though trying to warm me. I noticed the tremors jerking through my body. The twit thought I was cold. Unreal. Her smile grew so wide I hoped her head would split, spilling what passed for her brains onto the asphalt of the parking lot. "He's from Louisiana money, I heard. You hit the lotto, kid. She's a chip off the old block, all right." She pecked my cheek and exchanged a grin with Amanda. I fought to keep from wiping the dampness from her kiss off my face.

"Where's...Ron?" It took me a moment to remember her current husband's name.

"Who cares?" She exhaled a world-weary sigh. "The jerk traded me in for a newer model. His new lady is probably younger than you, Peri Jean. Of course, she's not nearly as pretty." She and Amanda laughed, reminding me of those cartoon crows Memaw thought were so funny. Barbie's phone buzzed, and she took it out of her handbag to glance at it. "I've got to get moving. That's the realtor. She's going to show me a cute little house."

Amanda quickly told Barbie about the natural anti-aging ingredients of the homemade lotion she was selling her, conveniently leaving out the way all her homegrown miracle cures smelled. Then she told her the price.

"Well, I sure hope it works." Barbie handed her two twenties.

"Oh, all my formulas do exactly what they're supposed to, right Peri Jean?" Amanda winked at me.

"They do." I didn't care to continue the conversation with Barbie, but Amanda wanted an endorsement. I had no choice but to give it. "I burned this hand last month at work. It blistered, puss ran out of it, the whole song and dance. Bought some of Amanda's herbal healing salve. Look here. Not even a red mark." I held out the hand for her to inspect. The way the wound healed really had impressed me. Amanda might act a little loopy, but she knew her stuff.

Barbie inspected my hand. "I'll take your word for it, but only because you're my baby girl." She walked toward her car but turned back before she reached it. "My cell number's still the same," she said. "Set up a time I can meet your honey. I am absolutely bursting with excitement. *Louisiana money,*" she muttered under her breath and walked to her car, actually throwing me a big wink before she got inside.

Once a gold digger, always a gold digger. I'd have laid down the twenty-dollar bill in my back pocket to bet Barbie's real interest in me had to do with Dean's family money. She probably thought she could worm her way back into my life instead of finding a new husband, which might be hard with her no longer being young. My foot itched to kick her departing behind, but she was gone, and I needed to act as professional as I could.

"The new washer won't be here until this afternoon," Amanda said. "I need you to get these towels over to the Laundromat and wash them." She took a closer look at me. "Are you all right, hon?"

I was, and I wasn't. For the life of me, I couldn't remember what I'd been so upset about when I drove over here. I remembered being at the museum with Hannah, making her angry because I didn't want to get crazy from the Mace Treasure on my shoes. But what had I been so upset about when I pulled into the beauty shop parking lot?

"Peri Jean, honey, you all right?" Amanda stepped closer and closed one of her strong hands around my arm. My knees weakened, and I listed to the side, black spots in my vision. Amanda got one arm around my waist and had me in the beauty shop before I could recover enough to protest.

Every face turned to me, eyes alight with curiosity. A few women tried to feign pity, but not very hard. I tried to pull myself together and fast. The gossip grapevine in Gaslight City could have competed in NASCAR. I didn't want to give any of these people an evening's entertainment. I fought to rein myself in, but my feelings welled up, flooding and overflowing the shallow reserves of my emotions. *How dare my awful mother act as though I'd let her swing back into my life?* I let the outrage the thought generated cancel out some of the hurt and immediately felt more stable.

Barbie acted as though she'd been on a long trip and we were picking up where we left off. Then the core of it hit me like a bucket of ice cold piss. In the depths of Barbie's artfully made up eyes had been nothing but confidence in her ability to win me over. She either had no idea how she'd made me feel all my life or didn't give a rat's ass.

I could get as mad as I wanted. I could act as much of a horse's ass as I wanted. It wouldn't touch Barbie. I could buy into her act whole hog and eat until I popped. No matter how nice I was, no matter how hard I tried, Barbie would dump me when it suited her. Inside, I sagged, the hurt pounding like a bad injury. Outside, I used every trick I'd learned to push a smile onto my face. I turned to Amanda.

"Sorry about that. Memaw had a bad night last night, and I'm tired."

I waited while all the woman in the shop clucked in sympathy. Hazel Siegler pushed the hair drying apparatus off her head and turned it off, leaning forward in the dryer chair to catch all the action.

"Sugar, I'll spend the night with Miss Leticia if you ever need a break," she said. "We worked together over at the high school together all our adult lives. It'd be just like a slumber party."

"Thank you, Miss Hazel. I'll sure keep it in mind." Problem was, Hazel lived at a nursing home because she couldn't care for herself. I turned to Amanda. "You still got a job for me?"

"I do." She patted my back. If I hadn't known better, I'd have said it was congratulations for pulling myself together. She led me into a side room, which held a washer and dryer. Piles of towels littered the floor. "You can do this however you want, but I need them out of here ASAP and washed today."

I knelt on the floor and began gathering towels, pushing them into a canvas bag I'd spotted hanging on the wall. Amanda leaned against the door frame and watched me.

"I never realized you and Barbie had issues."

"I didn't realize you and Barbie were such close friends." I finished loading the towels and slung the bag over my shoulder.

"We aren't." The lines around Amanda's eyes deepened into what would have been a smile had her mouth not remained still. "When she lived here, she came to me for haircuts. Came in here for a perm the day she left town. Never said a word about moving away." She moved away from the door. "Come on. I'll open the door for you and help you get them into your car."

I waddled through the shop, mulling over what Amanda said. It rang true in my ears. Maybe Barbie didn't really make friends. Too self-absorbed? Too conniving?

"What's she doing in here?" The raspy, squeaky voice jabbed into my thoughts like sharp ice.

I dropped the towels on the floor and turned to face its source, even though I knew exactly who'd spoken.

Felicia Brent Fischer Holze smirked at me from underneath her red-streaked mousy hair. She'd smeared oddly colored makeup over her angular features, and her gut had grown considerably since I'd last seen her. Either she'd made good friends with after-work beer drinking or she was pregnant again. I didn't care which it was. All I cared about was not doubling up my fist and hitting her with it. I got away with beating up my childhood tormentor once. It wouldn't happen again. She was married to a sheriff's deputy, and her father-in-law was the sheriff of Burns County. I had a feeling I wouldn't escape prosecution if I hit her.

"What's around your neck?" She took a few steps toward me and plucked the black opal from my shirt.

"Don't touch me, Felicia." I tightened my grip on the canvas bag holding the towels.

"Is it a substitute for an engagement ring on your finger?"

I turned my back to her and stood in front of the door. Amanda appeared next to me and held it open. She held my elbow as I took the step down onto the stoop.

"He's gonna lose, Peri Jean," Felicia sang after me. "Are y'all going to live out there in your Memaw's house and be jobless together?"

"That's enough, Felicia. We have customers." Amanda's voice brooked no argument. She followed me out of the shop.

"Thanks for ignoring her," she said when we reached my old Nova. "She's a good stylist, brings in a lot of clientele, but sometimes I could wring her neck."

"I'm glad I'm not the one who has to work with her." I handed Amanda the keys and let her pop the trunk.

"Sometimes you have to work with people you don't like because of who they're related to." Amanda stared at the Nova and ran her hand over the flank. I hefted the canvas bag into the trunk and closed it.

"I ever tell you how cool I think it is for you to drive your daddy's car?" Amanda stared at the street, eyes unfocused and misty. She didn't seem to expect an answer, so I didn't bother thinking of one. "Paul Mace. Your daddy was the best looking guy in town. He'd rev up the engine on this baby, and you could hear him a mile away." The corners of her mouth turned down. "Too bad he died so young."

Yep, too fucking bad. I kept the comment to myself and walked around to the driver's side door and waited for Amanda to dismiss me.

"Look…I hate it when people tell me what I ought to do, but right now I'm about to do it. Try to make friends with your mom. My situation growing up was a lot like yours. My mom left me for my grandmother to raise while she went off and got remarried."

I would rather bathe in hot garbage than open the door for Barbie to crucify my emotions.

"Did you make up with her?" I couldn't help asking. Amanda never, ever discussed her past, and it remained a mystery because she didn't grow up here.

"Nope. Last time I spoke to her, when I was about nine, I told her I hated her guts." Amanda took a breath and let it out. "She died two years later in a house fire. She, her new husband, and my half-brother."

Would I regret it if Barbie turned up dead? I didn't think so. I barely knew her, and what I did know was negative. But I could never be sure until the situation presented itself.

"Sometimes we forgive people, not to give them a pass for whatever wrong they committed against us or to get them to do a certain thing, but to be kinder to ourselves." Amanda watched my face and then nodded. She patted my arm. "Think about it. Okay?"

"I will." I opened the door climbed into the car. "I gotta get on this if I want to finish. Thanks for the talk."

"You bet." A car pulled into the parking lot, and Amanda walked over and talked to the person, following them inside her business, still chattering.

I started the car, a little fear tingling at me. I tried to remember why I'd been scared again, hoping it would come with Barbie gone, but I couldn't access it. It was gone, as though it had never been. Just as well. If it had to do with the Mace Treasure, I was better off forgetting it. I put the car in gear, and my cellphone rang. I checked the caller ID. Eddie Kennedy. *Uh oh.* "Hi, Eddie."

"What do you mean telling Hannah you can't help her? Don't you know what this is about?"

"Something I don't want any part in." I cringed as I said the words. Back talking Eddie felt wrong no matter how old I got.

"I want you to meet me at Hooty's."

"I have a job. I'll spend the day at the laundromat doing Amanda's towels from her beauty shop."

Eddie slapped his hand over the phone, nearly deafening me, and said a few things. I heard Hooty Bruce's deep voice answer.

"Hooty says bring the towels here. And, Peri Jean? Darlin'?"

"Yes?"

"Move your skinny ass."

End of Sample

Order Rocks & Gravel from your favorite bookseller.

ISBN: 978-1-947462-07-6

Visit Catie's website:
www.catierhodes.com

Find Catie on Facebook:
http://www.facebook.com/catierhodesauthor

Follow Catie on Book Bub.
https://www.bookbub.com/authors/catie-rhodes

Join Catie's email list:
http://smarturl.it/lrdenewsletter

ABOUT THE AUTHOR

Catie Rhodes writes southern-fried urban fantasy with a strong dose of horror and a side dish of humor.

She is the author of the Peri Jean Mace Ghost Thrillers. Her stories have appeared in *Tales From The Mist*, *Let's Scare Cancer to Death*, and *Allegories of the Tarot*.

Catie was born and raised behind the pine curtain in East Texas. She comes from a family of world champion liars.

Their tall tales molded Catie into a purveyor of her own brand of lies and legends. One day, she found the courage to start writing down her stories. It changed her life forever.

Catie Rhodes lives steps from the Sam Houston National Forest with her long-suffering husband and her armpit terrorist of a little dog.

Find me online:
www.catierhodes.com